Brutus Nation 3
Into the Fires of Hell

by Kris Kyzer

 FriesenPress

One Printers Way
Altona, MB R0G 0B0
Canada

www.friesenpress.com

Copyright © 2024 by Kris Kyzer
First Edition — 2024

All rights reserved.

No part of this publication may be reproduced in any form, or by any means, electronic or mechanical, including photocopying, recording, or any information browsing, storage, or retrieval system, without permission in writing from FriesenPress.

ISBN
978-1-03-831324-9 (Hardcover)
978-1-03-831323-2 (Paperback)
978-1-03-831325-6 (eBook)

1. FICTION, THRILLERS

Distributed to the trade by The Ingram Book Company

For settlers on Mars

Guts & Bolts

1 Hunt _____ 1

2 Twisted _____ 17

3 Combat _____ 29

4 Ruin _____ 43

5 Horizon _____ 53

6 Roach _____ 65

7 Conviction _____ 81

8 Moon _____ 93

9 Game Face _____ 105

10 Furnace _____ 117

11 Lava® _____ 131

12 Slayer _____ 141

13 Curtain _____ 155

Planet Kyzer _____ 165

1 Hunt

"Residents of Cowherd's Pike are urged to exercise extreme caution tonight, as the search is on for three escaped convicts from the Glendale Oax® penitentiary. The three men—ages twenty-eight, thirty-four, and forty-two—overpowered a pretzel truck driver and used his vehicle to slip past prison security. When asked what a pretzel truck was doing on the premises, Guvner Oscar Corrigan stated that the matter is being looked into with a magnifying glass but that most prison resources are focused on obtaining intel and bolstering security protocols. Even though they are likely unarmed, the men—pictured here—are extremely dangerous. They were last spotted near Glendale River, off Local Road 34. Residents should keep an eye out and report anything suspicious to the nearest law enforcement office or by calling 110. Up next, sports and weather. I'm Lin Wesley, wishing you a good night. Be vigilant, stay safe, and, as always, keep your eye on Channel 5®!"

As the anchorwoman pushed her chair back and stepped away from the desk, she clocked her manager, Rusty Blevins, chatting with one of the producers next to the kitchenette. She made her way toward them and stopped in front of the vending machine.

"Linselotte Wesley, as she stands and saunters!" Rusty said. "A magnificent performance. Sovereign!"

"Really? This again?" She reached into her pocket, took out a VendaKey®, and swiped it to unlock a half-liter can of Mocha

Muchachos® Original 2XCaff™ Sugar B-Gone™. The can tumbled out with a thud.

"So loud," she murmured.

"You'd think they'd find a way to make it less prol," the producer said, throwing in his two ass-lick cents.

"Idiots," Rusty concurred.

"Let's walk 'n' talk," Lin said. "Like in the movies."

"So alpha." Rusty grinned and then lock-stepped next to her. The producer peeled off.

"Oh, I just realized what I said there! 'Sovereign!' Ha! It wasn't planned. I swear."

"Easy does it." Lin slurped her coffee. "Just say what's on your mind."

"Yorba Woods sweetened the offer. Half a mil more."

She slowed down. "Why do they want me so bad?"

"Isn't it obvious? You're a rising star, yet untainted. Everyone else is either in prison or discredited."

"I don't want my breakout to be on the backs of all those victims."

"Victims?" Rusty cocked an eyebrow.

"The new viscount's.[1] Back when he was a criminal, remember?"

"Oh that." Rusty waved it away. "Never proven."

"Money can clean even the toughest stains."

"That may be so, but he's a sovereign now." Rusty shrugged. "And he wants to share his vision with the world."

"The feel-good story of the year." She gulped and glared at him.

"If you don't wanna . . ." He turned up his palms.

"Such a drama queen." She grinned. "I'll think about it. Happy?"

"Never happy. But happi**er** than five minutes ago."

1* Asterisks denote references to previous books in the series.

"Go ahead, say it!" Thomas "Tommy Lo" Lorenz said. "You think I've lost me bloody marbles—I'm a cert for the asylum."

Vincent "Lucky" Malanga Jr. shrugged. "It's just . . . it seems like overkill."

"It's **supposed** to! Shoot—to—thrill! Feel—the—kill!"

"Yeah, feel it deep in the ass . . ."

"Don't forget 'hard.'"

"Deep . . . deep and hard," Lucky murmured.

"Your lips say yes, but your heart says no."

"Which part of 'overkill' isn't clear?"

"Snake goes for pipe!" Tommy grabbed Lucky by the throat and pushed his mug into the shotgun side glass.

"Mmhmph . . ."

"Don't go foggin' up my window now!"

Lucky raised his arms, signaling surrender.

"Brothers to the end, right?"

"And the end will come tonight? We're twenty-five years old."

Tommy grabbed Lucky by the ears and got into his mug: "You . . . and I . . . will chase away the clouds . . . in the sky . . ."

"The fuck . . ."

"I want you to **want to** be a part of this. Part of history. Will you join me for a spot of history making on this misty night?"

Lucky shrugged. "Sure."

"Shoulder check!" Tommy opened the driver's door and then went to the back of the van. His buddy followed suit.

Tommy unlocked the back door and opened both wings. He did a quick scan of the area around them before unveiling the contents of a crate. "Feast your tired eyes on this."

Lucky's peepers popped. "The fuck is that?"

The AUIM off-roader glided across Local Road 34 as dusk was twilighting into sunset.

The navigation screen illuminated the interior, the radio crackling with updates.

Commander Zeb Simons kept his eyes on the road, occasionally glancing at the screen. Lieutenant Nina Paulson rode shotgun, scanning files for intel.

"Two minutes."

"Roger," Paulson replied. "All caught up."

"His dog's name?"

"Buff. But we don't know that, right?"

Simons smiled. "Gold star, Lieutenant."

Their destination was on the left side of the road. The off-roader made a U-turn and drove up a short path lined by trees.

They stopped in front of a one-story house surrounded by more trees and several sheds scattered about.

The officers exchanged glances. Simons nodded, then they exited the car.

The moon was bright as they made their way up the dusty approach to the house. The stairs creaked, the leaves hissed, and the porch wobbled.

Once in front of the greasy door with the oily window, Simons raised a clenched fist at Paulson.

She grinned. "Hammer of justice?"

"Not quite. But it'll do."

He slammed his RespirArmor®-wrapped glove into the door so hard and loud that it made Paulson jump.

"AUIM! Please come to the door!"

"One more hit like that, and this door is history," she low-voiced.

Simons paused and ear-strained. "I spy a distant noise. There might be some hope for the door yet."

"On the other hand, his file declares him a DIY dude. He might relish the challenge."

"No Magnussen & Melberg® for this guy? There's a shock."

"Here he comes now."

"Yeah. In all his glory."

After some heavy clanging noises, the door opened, and Hieronymus "Old Man" Kelski emerged. "Sorry about that. Had to disarm the boobie traps. Damn coyotes."

"You keep coyote traps inside your home?"

"Them bastards are number one worldwide in slipfuckery. Boundaries? They know none. They'll be nabbing peanuts out yer asshole if you so much as blink too long."

"I'm more of a coconut candy lady myself."

"To each his—**her**—own." Old Man Kelski tugged his forelock at Paulson.

"Commander Simons, Lieutenant Paulson, Interior Ministry." Simons thumb-pointed. "Mind if we take a minute of your time?"

"Got nuthin to hide." Kelski pulled up his denim overalls and planted his palms in his armpits.

"You might have heard about the prison escape? Three inmates busted out of Glendale earlier today."

Old Man Kelski nodded. "Go on."

"Based on our latest intel—information—we have reason to believe that the escapees might be hiding in the woods around your house."

"I know what 'intel' means," Kelski said.

"Mind if we take a peek? Just to make sure you're safe here?"

"Mighty noble of our esteemed Ministry to go all gaga for Old Man Kelski's well-being and all, but since when does the Ministry bother to ask for permission to go wood-creeping?"

"Not permission. More of a heads up. To avoid any potential unpleasantries."

"Blind duckling?"

"That would definitely be one of them."

"Well, if you gotta—horse on a cowboy, how come the critter didn't holla?"

"Critter, sir?"

Kelski whipped out a pair of binox from his front pouch. "The mutt, el perro."

He stepped onto the porch and pointed the binox toward one of the outlying sheds. "Sleeping peacefully," he murmured. "She's s'posed to holla when foreign folk approach. I oughta re-intro the belt into her life, refreshen the old Kelski Gospel." He shook his head. "That bitch has had it way too good for way too long."

"What's her name?"

Kelski returned the binox in his pouch. "Buff."

The cops remained silent.

"Y'all wanna go in them woods? Creep away! Hope you catch them scum. But I also hope you brought backup coz them woods is bigger than a hooker's hoo-ha."

"Local police, provincial police, the Ministry—we're all pitching in."

"What happened to small government?" Kelski grinned.

"It grew bigger."

"Spinach subsidies."

Simons head-pointed at Paulson. "Rim shot! Good job, Lieutenant!"

"Guess WAWA[2] was good for something after all." Kelski stepped back into the house.

"Just one more point to clarify, sir." Simons fiddled with his wrist-comm.

"Can't a fella watch his neckeddies in peace? I told you, go knock yourself out in them woods! I won't take you fer rustlers."

---

2   WAWA: Women Are Welcome Act of 1953, which granted women the right to vote in all elections and to run for public office. It also removed all legal barriers to their entry into any profession.

"Did anything strike you as odd when you heard about the breakout?" Simons asked.

"Like what?"

"The fact that one of the prisoners is a cousin of yours."

"No. He's a go-getter."

His go-getting got him ten years for mail fraud, Paulson thought. "When did you last have contact with Klenny?"

"'Have contact'? I don't swing that way, no siree. Old Man Kelski is all manski."

Did he just wink at me? Paulson wondered. She decided to rephrase it. "When did you last speak to Klenny?"

He sighed. "Must be years. I like that boy, only . . . Me and his side of the family don't keep in touch much. Sad."

"He got transferred to Glendale some six months ago. He never reached out to you?"

"Never. As far as I heard. And I woulda gone to see him."

"You referred to the escapees as 'scum' a minute ago," Simons pointed out. "But now you say you like Klenny?"

"I meant the other two."

"I see."

"But I do hope you catch 'em all. Klenny too. Don't come knockin' on this heart of mine if your ass is wearing that orange jumpsuit."

"Before we hit the woods, is there anything else you want to share with us regarding your cousin?" Simons asked. "Any piece of information that might help us locate him?"

"No. Look, hey now, wait a minute. Is that the real reason why y'all came to disturb old Kelski in his man-castle out here? It had nuthin to do with no goddamn trail leading into no woods, did it? You twos think old Kelski's hiding them boys."

"You're not a suspect, Mr. Kelski. It's a mere precaution. There are three prisoners on the run, and one of them happens to be a relative of yours. He might decide to pay you a visit, force you into helping him. And their last known route indicated they were heading this way."

"Right." Kelski hocked a loogie not far from where Simons was standing. "The big, bad woods."

"How—where will you hide this thing?"

"That's what **she** said. And I ain't even **trying** to hide it, bruv."

Tommy and Lucky stood at the back of Tommy's van—actually, the van belonged to Tommy's girlfriend's sister's boss—going over that night's battle plan. More precisely, Tommy was thinking out loud while Lucky was doing his best to hold on to a shred of dignity as he was being dragged kicking and screaming (or at least quietly whimpering) thru another trademark Tommy Lorenz big-leagues-or-bust roll of the dice.

"You think you'll be able to reach the target without anyone stopping you? While carrying this?"

"'Target.' I like the sound of that. You're finally getting into the spirit of Operation Constipated Seagull."

Lucky couldn't help but laugh. The sound of a gallows pole-bound sod. The evening was escalating in bizarreness on an alarming scale.

"Okay, so let's say you get to him. Then what? You'll use this thing on him? For real?"

"That's how you move up in this patch of the world."

"That's how you end up in the hole! Or a hole in the ground."

"While you're writing poems, I'll get Blazin' Bessie ready." Tommy attached a stainless-steel canister to the bottom of the Strechler® F99 flamethrower. "Krunk! Let Mars sort them out."

"It has a name, I see."

"'It' is a 'she,' you rube. First rule of self-defense: your weapon shall have a girl's name."

Lucky's mug went blank. "Self-defense? It's a goddamn **flamethrower**."

"Anything less would be an insult to gangland gods."

"I've known you since kindergarten. You ain't a gangster."

"Right, and you've been riding my coattails ever since kindergarten." Tommy grinned. "Have I ever steered you wrong?"

"You've steered me into prepping a terror attack. So, yes."

"Would you listen to the drama? This is no more than your local neighborhood boys-will-be-boys Friday night steam release."

"It's Saturday."

Tommy bumped Lucky on the shoulder. "I knew I kept you around for a reason."

"If it's just another Friday/Saturday night, what's Blazin' Bessie doing here?"

"Tommy Lo always goes big. That's why he's never home."

Lin Wesley beep-beeped her SherzKex® SUV open, placed a plastic bag on the shotgun seat, threw her purse on the backseat, then sat behind the wheel.

Mirror—check. Hair—check. Teeth—check. Lipstick—check. Sensor—check. Good to go. Time to roll.

She maneuvered the car out of the Channel 5® underground parking garage and was soon cruise-speeding down Interprovincial 26, Ploughburg's lights blurring around her.

She had gotten the coveted 9 p.m. news anchor nod after her predecessor was exposed as a member of a Psychoward* ring. The network kept the information to themselves to avoid a scandal. The press release stated the reason for his departure was a burning desire to spend more time with his family.

At the time, Lin was a rising star at Channel 2®'s Stavenage office, although she wasn't an anchorwoman yet. The call from Channel 5® came as a surprise not just to her but also to veteran industry watchers, most of whom suspected bed-poling. And yet she hadn't greased a single wheel with her tongue or her wallet. One year into her Channel 5® tenure, she had the best numbers in a hundred-mile radius.

Suck on that pole, haters.

She had just hit thirty, was in scrumptious shape (a Stavenage nine and a Ploughburg ten), interviewing nothing but DREQ 400 hotshots for the boyfriend role, captaining her semi-pro volleyball team to the national semis (coming up in two weeks' time) and making her way thru the twelve-volume collected works of Anton Zhlubregitsin.

And yet, a cloud was casting a dark shadow over it all. Her manager's pestering efforts had been growing in volume and frequency. A powerful man was demanding a TV interview, waving obscene piles of zalers at her, and she wasn't sure how much longer she could keep him at bay.

Perhaps the powers that be had decided to cash in a favor she didn't even know she owed.

"Commander Simons! I need a sitrep on the Kelski woods, over."

Kelski grinned. "Mommy's mad?"

Simons smiled back at Kelski, then spoke into his watch-com. "Permission to search cleared, Command. Send in the shovels, over."

Old Man Kelski didn't like the sound of that. "Did my one good ear just do a double take? Did y'all go mentioning some sharp and pointy shovels now?"

The commander shook his head. "'Shovels' as in 'search troops.' We won't disturb the pristineness of the forest."

"You won't even know we were there," the lieutenant added, doubling down.

"Did you just wink at me?" Kelski's cojones were growing bigger by the minute.

She laughed and was about to retort when they heard a metal-on-metal sound from the basement.

The two AUIMers immediately went into "us against the world" mode, drawing handguns and advancing into the living room. Simons directed Kelski to sit on the couch and not move. Paulson plastered herself next to the basement door and grabbed the handle.

"AUIM! I'm about to open the door to the basement! Stand back!"

She turned the knob and pushed the door open.

"Whoever is down there, identify yourselves!"

"There ain't no one down there, dang fools. 'Less it's coyotes. In which case—"

"Sure. I can hear the howling all the way up to here." Simons made a throat-cutter gesture at Kelski, who leaned forward on the couch but remained seated.

"Klenny?" Paulson called down into the basement. Silence.

"Klenn**yyyyy?**"

Silence.

"Hope you had your fun with them girly guns of yours. I told you there weren't no ghosts and goblins down there." Old Man stood up and pointed at his crotch. "Wanna see a real man's gun?"

"I will start a countdown from five! If you don't identify yourself by the time I reach one, we are authorized to use lethal force!"

Both cops cocked their guns and pointed them at the doorway.

"Five!"

"Don't shoot, for fuck's sake. We're coming out."

Simons swept Old Man's feet, jammed a knee into his back, and slapped on the cuffs.

"Keep your hands high and clear! I wanna see all ten fingers gleaming!" Paulson yelled at the perps as they exited the basement.

Once all three were in the living room, she told them to get on their knees and palms-on-top-of-head it, then Simons cuffed them.

Old Man Kelski turned his neck as much as he could, seeming genuinely shocked at the sight in his house. "Klendrick Kelski, you schemin' imbecile! Bringin' the law to my home? Trying to drag me into your mud? What in tarnation is malfunctioning in that pea-sized brain of yours?!"

"Command, the targets are in custody! We got all three of them. This is Commander Simons live and uncut from the Kelski house off Local Road 34. I repeat, the targets are in custody. Backup not critical but appreciated. Simons out."

"Copy, Commander. The shovels were already dispatched. They'll help haul away the precious cargo. Outstanding work."

"Pig or bear? No, the bear one is lame. How about a croc? Or President Martin?"

Tommy was trying to decide which mask to wear during the night's festivities.

"Wait, don't you want them to know it was you?" Lucky asked.

"I want the streets to know it was me, but I don't want the cops to be able to **prove** it was me."

"Master of illusion over here."

"I hope you're learning, my young apprentice."

"Stop calling me that!"

"Oh, so **now** he decides to grow a pair." Tommy pointed at a mask that was easier for Lucky to reach. "Hand me that Owls[3] mask."

---

3   Scowling Owls® of Stavenage: Stavenage's APL® (Athenian Pixkin League) franchise. The team draws its identity from the city's rich university heritage.

Lucky hesitated.

Tommy was about to bust out the snake again, only to realize why Lucky had frozen. "My young apprentice is worried he'll leave fingerprints? Make John Ebenezer Law descend upon the Malanga residence, copters and all?"

"Well . . . yeah. What if you get . . . neutralized?"

"I might get neutralized, but I'll never get neutered. Subtle hint." Tommy pointed at Lucky's crotch.

Lucky pulled his jacket sleeve over his hand, then grabbed the mask and handed it to his buddy. "How come there's all this stuff in here?"

"I was wondering when you'd ask. The van owner's a carnie. He—no, his brother's the carnie. And the owner sometimes lets him use the van for . . . carnie matters."

"Uh-huh."

"There's an inflatable bearded lady somewhere in there, 'case you get lonely."

"Why would they make—ah, man, shut the fuck up."

Lin Wesley was ten minutes away from her destination when her cell phone interrupted the pleasant SherzKex® Pure Platinum™ engine hum.

She snuck a peek at the number and answered in a mock sitcom voice. "Who else but Rusty!"

"Who loves ya, Linny? **Everybody,** of course! Say it with me: **every**—"

"Rusty."

"Nah, I just thought it could be a new thing. I say, 'Who loves ya, Linny,' and you go 'Everybody.' No, we both go **'Everybody'**—"

"Rusty, stop tromboning."

"As madam wishes. And clever."

"Thank you. How can Ploughburg and environs' number-one newscaster help you on this misty night?"

"Just wanted to newsflash you: they got the escapees. The Ministry did. Old Man Kelski's house. I'm sure the network will be wall-to-walling it tomorrow."

"Old Man Kelski? Should that name ring a bell?"

"I keep forgetting you're still new around these parts. He's a local celebrity, stubborn as a mule and as smelly as a stool."

"Cool."

Rusty laughed. "Seems he was lending a helping hand to his nephew or something. One of the three convicts."

"Alright. Thanks for the info. I'll get on the prep first thing tomorrow. Well, later today, as it's past midnight."

"Eye for detail. That's my Lin!"

"Am I disconnecting? The rest of my pretzels are getting cold."

"Pretzels? You bought pretzels after the show?"

"Yep. Get It Twisted™—Our Pretzels Pack A Punch!™"

"Wait, one of their trucks was used in the escape."

"Correct. They have a kiosk in the lobby of our building. Never tried 'em until today. Not bad at all. In fact, it just might be my new go-to pretzel place. If that's a thing."

"Nothing like a nationally televised prisoner hunt to raise brand awareness."

"Organic eyeballs."

"I wonder if they deliver."

"Ta-daaah!"

Lucky stood and watched as Tommy showed off his outfit but said nothing.

"Hard of hearing? **Ta-daaah!**"

"Yell louder, why dontcha? Another criminal mastermind who can't help broadcasting his schemes."

Tommy dismiss-waved his gloved hand and pointed the flamethrower at the driver's door. "You no longer amuse me, jester in training. Go sit while real men clash like the titans they are."

"If I ain't a real man, how come I'm about to cuddle up with an inflatable bearded lady?"

"Ha! These mean streets might make a jester out of you after all."

Tommy pulled the Scowling Owls® mask over his mug, gripped the Strechler F99 with both hands, and turned to leave. "Tell my not-yet-conceived son I did this to make the world a better place."

"You're not planning to return?"

"Ideally, I'd love to return. But titan clashes tend to be . . . fateful."

2 Twisted

"**Leo!**"

Leo von Abzuger opened his eyes and felt his heart start to jog.

"You don't honestly think [inaudible] all day in [inaudible] while I play the part of a servant, do you?"

Her voice was floating in and out while she zipped around on her broom, simultaneously scolding Leo for his Sunday morning bed wallowing and keeping him up to date on the delicate dynamics of the local glitterati scene.

"I don't even understand how a grown-ass man can allow himself to let the precious weekend minutes tick away like this. I tried to—are you listening to me?—I tried to call the Boltons; that is, I **did** call them, but no one answered. No callback either. Beginning to suspect we're being left out of the loop. Falling behind. That's how it starts. Phone call return ratio starts to dip. Then the dinner invitations start getting scarce. 'Must be the new mailman.' Right, it's a conspiracy down at the post office. The people there have nothing better to [inaudible] the von Abzuger invitations. [Inaudible] the years I've known them. Next, the golf charity tourney is allegedly overflowing with celebs, so there's no need for our participation, thank you a million. Eternal gratitude. Like those [inaudible]. And then there's the weddings."

There was a pause of about thirty ticks.

Did she go downstairs?

Closer to the bedroom: "Don't even get me started on the weddings."

No, still on the top floor.

"Are you still horizontal in there? **Leo!** Don't tell me I'm dropping these nuggets to an empty audience! These pearls of wisdom and wit. I should get into podcasting . . ."

She trailed off, and Leo turned over on his back. Another day in the von Abzuger residence off to a rickety start.

He had returned from his Kittay exile* about three years ago and settled in Costa Aurelia, as planned. What wasn't planned was hooking up with a socialite on a mission to bust back into the Stavenage high society after her ex-husband's fall from grace had knocked her a few pegs down the ladder. Mercifully, her two grown kids lived on far-away college campuses, so the only krach in the house came from her. Not that she needed any help with krach.

"Did you speak to the phone company?"

Phone company?

"No, what—oh yeah, the interwebs. Yeah, I did." Leo had no energy for a yellathon.

"You wouldn't be trying to turn me into a coaxer again, would you? **Would you?**"

"He said they'll send someone next week. The problem is somewhere outside. Not in the house."

"Outside of what? The house?"

"Goddamn, yes, that's what I said. Where are you now?"

[inaudible]

"Come in here so we can talk normal! I don't wanna yell back and forth!"

"Normal**ly.**" Bellagrazia von Abzuger nee Fontucci ex-Nelson entered the room.

"*That* she hears," Leo mumbled, then turned onto his other side.

"Reel back that move. The wheels are rolling at ten hundred hours, maggot."

18 Kris Kyzer

"Aye-aye, Sergeant." Leo touched his temple in a mock salute and then turned over on his back again.

"These stripes say 'colonel,' you grunt. Drop and give me ten."

"Only ten? Mis-ranking carries a penalty of at least fifty."

"I don't want you all heart-attacky. Not yet."

Leo guffawed. "What's that smirk supposed to mean? Huh?" He lunged out of bed, grabbed her by the butt, and pulled her toward him. They tongue-twisted for a minute, followed by a brief loving-eye gaze.

He stepped away from her and was once again floored by how well she was holding up. She had been celebrating her forty-ninth birthday for a few years now but still looked finger-licking good.

"I have a good mind to bend you over right here and now."

"But you can't. No time left." Beli smiled.

Leo sighed. "These dang junkets."

"If only."

"The company's paying, ain't it?"

"And who owns the company?"

"I do. **We** do."

She smooched and butt-slapped him. "In the shower you go."

"But I don't wanna . . ." Leo hung his head and then shuffled off to the small bathroom attached to the master bedroom and peeled off his jammies.

After pulling a fiddler on the faucet, he entered the tub and planted himself under the OceanFlood® blast of freshness. *Oh yeah, that's the stuff.*

He closed his eyes and stood there, enjoying the water's restorative powers as the night's grime was washed away in a hail of steam. After twirling beneath the showerhead, he reached for his trusty Pamper Me Gently® Clean+Serene™ For Men CharcoalCharge™ shower gel but grabbed only air.

As he pulled a squinter in search of the gun-metallic tube, a shadow loomed over his left side and came toward his face.

"**Aaah!**" Leo bounced off to his right and smacked his shoulder on the hot tile.

With his ticker boom-booming, he scrambled to fend off the threat while simultaneously trying to maintain uprightness in the slippery tub. "Who goes there?!"

"It's me, you dolt," Beli said, her voice muffled by the steam. "I brought you the new gel tube."

Leo exhaled and turned off the faucets, his heart rate returning to normal. "Blessed be the wicked. You nearly gave me a terminal one there."

"Blessed . . . **what?!**"

Leo slid-opened the shower door. "Never mind. As long as I got my resupply."

"Why'd you freak out like that?"

"I was floating on a cloud of foofy fluffiness. And then I saw this." He made a lizardry gesture with his arm. "I thought they sent a snake to do me in. Trained snake. Like in the movies. Maximum deniability."

"They?"

"The investors."

"How would they get their money back if you're dead?"

"Once I'm gone, they can install someone else to run things."

"Someone with a brain, you mean?"

"Hey!" He grabbed the shower gel tube from her. "Old Leo is still good for a surprise or two. The rodeo ain't over as long as this heart is beating. Despite your attempts to shut it down."

"Perhaps metaphors should be left to the pros?"

"First off, my eyes are **up here.**" Leo wiggled the tube in front of his mug. "And second—"

"Don't call me Shirley?"

"Thanks for the gel. You can see yourself out." He slid the shower door shut.

Timothy Phillips stared at the figures in disbelief.

The it-seems-too-good-to-be-true kind of disbelief.

If the digits were accurate, lives would be changed. Visions rewarded. Legacies cemented. Including his own.

He stared some more. He leafed thru the file front to back and back to front. He saw no gap in the fence.

Of course, a plan was just that—a plan. And life had a way of torpedoing plans. Like it torpedoed his dream of building a wealth-management company when assassins took out the CEO and his family.* To this day, it still seemed like something out of a bad dream.

He pressed the intercom. "Margie, how are the meeting odds looking?"

"Based on the latest intel from the big guy's assistant," his secretary replied, "he might be able to squeeze you in this evening. But she can't confirm it yet."

"Bet he's doing a spot of squeezing on that assistant, if you get my flow."

Silence.

"You there?"

"Yes, sir, still here."

"Not even a chuckle?"

"It's a different time."

"Angling for a raise?"

"My fishing pole seems to have gotten legs."

"Ha ha! See? I laugh at **your** stuff." Tim grabbed his blazer, which was draped over the back of his executive chair. "Thinking of heading out to Tornado. Any wishes?"

"Oh, lovely. Yes, a crispy chicken salad with garlic bread on the side. No, make that grilled chicken."

"**That'll** save you," Tim murmured, still fumbling with the blazer.

"Sorry, sir?"

"One healthy and nutritious meal coming up! If I ever untangle this jacket from hell."

"Is my help needed?"

"Nah, I got it." He shook the blazer a couple of times, crumb-checked it, then put it on. On his way out of the office, he mirror-glanced to make sure his appearance meshed with the RED ORE® ethos. *Wouldn't want to have to sit thru another employee seminar on the Right Way or the Highway*™.

He saluted Margie on his way to the elevator, then passed a few fellow execs on their way to and from lunch. All of them were wearing the same kind of blazer as him—navy blue light wool fabric with the RED ORE® logo on the left chest and their name and job title on the right. The uniform was a big part of the company's identity and overall vibe.

Founded over a hundred years ago by Mickel "Red Ore" O'Reilly, it had become the biggest Athenian energy behemoth of them all. As a former military man, O'Reilly had infused his baby with a set of values and principles, which mirrored the AUAF Code—honor, loyalty, grit, shrewdness, vision. The employees were meant to wear the uniform with pride and reflect it in their bearing. An unpresentable appearance was cause for termination. This included a rumpled blazer or a "slouchy demeanor." People had actually been fired over it. Tim had joined RED ORE® just under three years ago and was still considered a new mug (some of his lateral colleagues had been with the firm for their entire career). Therefore, he never took any chances when it came to blazers and bearing.

Just before Tim reached the elevator, he spotted the King of All Engineers and picked up the pace. It was vital that he not speak to him before meeting with the head honcho. As his schemes and dreams grew in scope and achievability, he found it more challenging to keep all the pieces in their proper place. Such was the life of a fledgling puppet master.

Not that he was complaining. At least he finally had a dream to chase. As a survivor of decade-long corporate counter-intel trench warfare, he knew not to get his hopes up. But he could definitely see a ray of light shining from above.

The King of All Engineers was all-businessing it down the elevator galleria, undoubtedly on his way to another miraculous workaround, when he was bumped into by Lexi from Insulation. As she chatted him up, the King seemed to perk up, giving Tim just enough room to slip by unnoticed.

He jumped into one of the elevators and rode it to underground level two. He had recently figured out that it took less time to walk to his go-to lunch spot from the garage entrance than from the lobby. He could have had the food delivered to his office, but he liked to stretch his pegs and air out his brain at least once a day.

The air was mild, but that didn't mean much. The Magma[4] weather was notoriously fickle, with snowstorms and heat blasts sometimes occurring within hours of each other. Still, Tim liked it there. Much more than he thought he would. Granted, he thought he would hate the place, so the bar was low. When he was offered the job, his image of Magma was that of a giant rock spewing smoke. Athenia's chimney, as it were.

Boy was I wrong.

Muskeg was a jewel, a burgeoning high-tech soon-to-be megastar of a city, proudly flexing its petrozaler muscle. Everything seemed shiny and new. There were more cranes than towers in its downtown core, and those cranes were raising ever grander 'scrapers.

Muskeg owed a lot of its good fortune to the rivalry between RED ORE® and We Haul Gas®. The arms race in which the two giants

---

[4] Magma: Situated in the north of the Athenian Union, Magma is the country's richest natural resources province. It borders Norlandum to the Northwest and Hylands to the Southeast. Muskeg, the capital, is where most of Athenia's energy companies are based.

engaged had resulted in many major breakthrus, some coming as recently as last week, according to the report Tim had seen that day.

He reached Taco Tornado®, but streuth!—there was a five-deep line. As he mulled which other snack spot to hit, he sensed someone's eyes on his back. He whipped his neck to his right and met a grinning gaze.

"I've been eye-piercing you from the moment you turned the corner!" the man called out to him. "Where's your sixth sense?"

Tim walked over to the bench where the man was sitting. "In the shop."

"I went ahead and ordered your chalk." The man, known to Tim only as the Source, pointed to the bundle next to him. "Crunchy chicken and tangy pickles."

"I also need a salad for Margie."

"Let's stroll to that all-natural place. There's never a line there."

Leo slapped some cologne on his cheeks and exited the bathroom. "Refreshed and re . . . Beli?"

There was no sight or sound of her, so he assumed she was waiting for him downstairs. He went to the walk-in closet and opened it. A man was standing inside, dressed in a dark suit. Leo screamed and sprang backward, landing on his butt and bumping his head on the bed. Just as he was about to roll away in panic, he glanced at the closet and realized no one was standing there. It was merely his own suit draped over a couple of hangers.

As he regained his breath and wobbled to his feet, he heard Beli running to the second floor. As she burst into the room, he sheepish-smiled and waved her away. "Sorry, babe. Got scared of my own shadow. Literally." He pointed to the closet.

"Oh, so now they sent a hitman, eh? In a snazzy suit."

"Fascinating how the mind works."
"Or doesn't."
"I heard that."
"I hope so."

She entered the closet and flicked on the light. "Last time you told me you got confused with how I displayed your outfit, so I adjusted the system. One hanger for the pants, one hanger for the shirt and blazer. All neatly arranged."

Leo rubbed the back of his head. "I think I'm getting a bump back here."

Beli took the clothes off the hangers and laid them on the bed. "There." She double-pointed: "Wear. This."

"Very droll." Leo bee-swallowed. "But seriously, please stop trying to kill me with a scare-induced heart attack."

She glided toward him, smiling. "I am your wife, so of course I'll kill you. One way or another." She smooched him on the forehead. "But not today. Today there are investors to charm."

"Don't I know it." His mug dropped.

"That frown? Turn it upside down and join me in the car."

"Aye, aye, sir."

"These new double taco wraps? Not half bad." The Source bit off a big chunk and nodded in approval.

"What are they exactly?" Tim asked. "Taco shells wrapped around a burrito?"

"Kinda. Hard on the outside, soft on the inside. Like yours truly."

"Right. I've known you for a year. You still don't wanna tell me your name."

"Ain't no better name than the Source. Like a superhero. If I told you my civvy name, you'd lose all respect for me over how bland it is."

Tim crunched on his crunchy chicken in silence.

"And honestly, Tim old boy . . ." The Source lowered his voice as they passed a group of interns, recognizable by their yellow blazers. "I figured you'd suss it out by now."

"You told me—" Tim caught himself mid-sentence and lowered his voice. "You told me not to even attempt to do that. Or you'd vanish in a puff of smoke."

"I am a bit of a drama queen, ain't I?"

Tim pulled an eye-roller.

"Well then." The Source finished his taco concoction and overhanded the balled-up wrapper into a trash bin. "Get ready for the most dramatic moment of all."

"I was wondering what the trench coat was for."

The Source covered his mug as his shoulders shook with laughter, then wiped away his laughter-tears. "Glad to see you've kept your sense of humor. Especially with what's at stake here."

"Only the future of the company. And the country."

"Right. Peanuts."

"Still hungry, are we?"

The Source produced a key from inside his coat. Tim pocketed it.

"Muskeg Bus Terminal 9. Locker 317. It's been a gas."

The Source crossed the road and headed for the subway station. Tim hurried back to his office, Margie's salad in hand.

Leo von Abzuger stopped the off-roader in front of the Copper Vale Golf Resort® entrance, opened the door, and reluctantly left the cozy confines of his Divota® 600B™.

After handing over the key and a tip to the valet, he took Bellagrazia under his arm and mustered up his best captain of industry stride as they made their way to the meeting room on the second floor.

The golf club was usually his oasis, but not today. "Lamb to the slaughter over here."

"It'll be fine. As long as you talk up the good trends."

"It's all smoke and mirrors. They'll see right thru me. These are some hard-assed nobody's fools."

"It. Will. Be. Fine." Beli pulled a nail-spur on his hand.

"What was I thinking? Edgy pretzels?! People like me should be put out of their misery."

"People like you built this country."

"So we have something to tear down."

They reached the door.

"Broad smile."

Leo tested his version of said smile on Beli.

"Or not." She tightened his tie.

"No good?"

"You look like a mental patient."

"Might as well be."

"Deep breath," Beli instructed. They both inhaled. "And exhale."

Leo turned the knob, and the two of them entered the room to a raucous cheer.

They exchanged puzzled looks.

"It seems they know something we don't," Leo muttered.

3 Combat

"The time . . . **has cooooome** . . ."

The crowd erupted in a wall-shaking roar as the announcer said the four magic words every MMA fan knew and loved.

". . . for the ACF® Brundell vs Haskin[5] main event!"

He waited for the noise to subside.

"This bout is brought to you by Mocha Muchachos®, the official caffeine partner of the ACF®. Mocha Muchachos®: Have a Cup, Grow a Pair!™ And by BLOODBOIL® 4: Heart Pumps Death™. Experience the ultimate revenge quest in BLOODBOIL® 4, available now on GameJoy® and GameJoy® ToGo™."

The announcer pointed to the CheezeeCubez® corner. "Fighting out of the Tundra, weighing in at two hundred and twenty pounds, sporting a record of fifteen wins and one loss, his eyes are dead and his rage is red, Rick 'the Hylandic Assassin' **Haaaaaaskin!**"

The Tax?GimmeABreak!® Arena showered the challenger with obligatory boos and may-your-kids-die-slowly well-wishes.

The announcer turned to the PeanutPoppers® corner. "Fighting out of Athenia City, weighing in at two hundred and sixteen pounds, with a record of eighteen wins and four losses, where his

---

5　ACF®: Athenian Combat Federation. Athenian Union's premier mixed martial arts organization. They hold monthly events, with Athenia City hosting a few of them each year, including that night's Brundell vs. Haskin Fueled by Mocha Muchachos® event.

fist ends, your nightmare begins, the reigning, defending ACF® light heavyweight champion of the world, Bobby 'Risen from Hell' **Brundeeeeeell!**"

The crowd's reaction out-decibeled all other ones that evening. It might have been the loudest thing Neil Zorich had ever heard. Sitting in a fifth-row VIP seat, he turned to his current BFF, Luke O'Reilly. "Your boy looks in primo shape! But this Haskin is one mean SOB!"

"Assassin my assin!" Luke retorted. "Bobby will eat his lunch!" He leaned in on Neil's ear. "Before I eat her twat."

He was referring to Anna "Athenia's Number One Bachelorette" Olkin, sitting next to him and covering her ears from the thundering noise. Neil chuckled, but his heart wasn't in it. There was only one man who should have been on that girl's twat duty, and his name was Neil Zorich.

"Perhaps we could give you a break on lumber subsidies. Or sweeten the old age pot."

The Central Government representative (CGR) was trying to lure in Cynthia Lennox ex-Holman* with token enticers.

"What if we took on some of the Hylands' fishery fund obligations?" Cynthia asked. "They're always moaning about it."

The CGR waved it off. "It's all for show. They're using it as a chip in the Frindesco® cleanup bargaining."

"What a mess that is."

"Don't I know it." The CGR tapped a cabinet drawer behind her desk.

"Is that . . . that's filled with Frindesco® files?"

"To the brim. And that's only the stuff related to my neck of the regulatory woods. There are probably thousands more files in various drawers."

"Poor trees."

"Very droll." The CGR smirked at Cynthia over her glasses.

"Ultra high-speed internet? We could install it out of our own pocket."

"You could? We're talking billions here. And part of it was already paid thru your Emerging Tech Chest contributions. The CG won't relinquish any of your tax channels in return for a one-off payment of a few billion, even if you could swing it."

"According to our research, Yorba Woods has more per-square logging potential than all of Hylands. Three times more, to be precise. And twice as much as Norlandum. Four times more than Herzland. If we could take—"

The CGR held up her palm. "It might be more per square, but it's a drop in the ocean when you take into account the size of those places. And also, 'potential.' I've seen it time and time again. Everyone gets all moist when they learn about the juicy deals available on lumber, but when it comes to implementing the necessary steps, they're a goner like a runner."

"Speaking of the ocean, how are the Western regions doing on carbon caps?"

"A-ziggin' and a-zaggin' today, are we?"

Cynthia shrugged. "Exploring all options."

"You don't need the government to trade carbon credits. It's a free market—well, free-**ish.** If you want, I can put you in contact with Gary from the Board[6] to give you a crash course in navigating the murky waters of nature nurture. But again, even if you take on all of Athenia's dirty air, you won't get to keep all those lovely taxes."

"You guys want them all, don't you?"

---

6   Athenian Energy Board: the country's top energy sector regulator, headquartered in Harrington.

The CGR smiled. "We feed on them."

Heading into the third of five scheduled rounds, Brundell seemed gassed.

He huffed and puffed as his corner bigged him up and patched his cuts. His mug was bloody and his right eye half closed from a spreading bruise. He was on his third mouthguard, the previous two having fallen victim to a hook and a knee. Had that knee landed full on, it would have been "sweet dreams, Bobby" in the first round. He did land a few of his trademark Brundell Bombs, but Haskin was not only still standing; he was also ahead on points due to landing even bigger blows of his own, the latest of which had seriously wobbled the champ.

Neil turned to his buddy. "Will he live to see the fourth?"

Luke seemed worried. "This fuckin' Haskin . . . made of stone."

"Pure Tundra granite."

"Fuck you," Luke laughed as Neil snuck a peek at Anna's mouth-watering neckline.

"This might be it," Neil said as the fighters emerged from their corners. "End of an era."

"Come on, Bobby baby, you got this!" Luke joined the down-but-not-out crowd in trying to boost the hometown hero. "Limb from limb, Bobby! Tear him limb from limb!"

"Have you given tourism any more thought?" the CGR tried going down a route they had traversed previously.

"Too flaky for the viscount's taste," Cynthia said. "Visitors come and go. What if they never return? He wants something more . . . tangible. Long term. Something that can't be taken away on a whim."

"CG doesn't operate that way." The CGR pulled a chest-puffer. "No whims. A deal's a deal. But so far I'm not hearing anything to write home about."

"I know this is an obvious one, and we touched on it earlier, but what about casinos? Las Islas is no longer a guaranteed cash cow now that Kittay has opened more to the world. A lot of gaming operators down there are hurting, and some have shuttered. Maybe they'd be willing to give Yorba a look."

"How is that not tourism?"

"Granted, you need visitors to come to your casinos, but it's not like only out-of-towners gamble. Locals would partake too."

"You don't need us for that."

"Not directly, but perhaps a quid pro quo where we build casinos and send all of their tax revenue to Harrington. In return, we get to keep our personal and business taxes."

"You have managed to intrigue me." The CGR pulled out her cell phone and started pressing buttons. "Just wanna see something here . . ."

Cynthia pointed to the monitor on the desk. "No big screen for you?"

"It's slow." She thumbed thru the phone. "The PC, that is. They were supposed to fix it." She chortled. "Five weeks and counting."

"Bums."

"Big time." The CGR looked at her phone in silence. "I'm sure my overlords will find a reason to torpedo it, but it's worth exploring."

"Impasse? Broken!" Cynthia slapped her palms. "And it only took us," she glanced at the clock on the wall, "six hours?! You gotta be kidding me."

"Time flies when you're crunching numbers and munching . . . what **are** we munching?"

Cynthia leaned back in her chair and closed her eyes. "I see . . . a red door . . ."

"This is a new one," the CGR remarked.

"A red door with a green lantern . . . or is it a hat?" Cynthia pressed her fingers against her temples. "No, not a hat. A mushroom! It's the world-famous Pepe's Pizza® mushroom logo!" She opened her eyes and grinned. "Extra-large Sundried Tomato Sunrise™ thin crust, anyone?"

The CGR sarcasti-clapped. "Bra-voh."

The Hylandic Assassin jumped on top of the cage wall and raised the ACF® light heavyweight championship belt over his head. He held it there for a good minute, soaking up the jeers rolling down from the stands. Then he grabbed the belt with his right hand and thumped his chest with his left, all the while spouting words of self-aggrandizing wisdom, which raised the crowd's disgust level to eleven.

"Aaass-hole gooo-home!" they chanted, which only spurred the new champ to even greater taunting heights.

He jammed the belt into his face and proceeded to tongue the ACF® logo. That stunt triggered a booing crescendo, followed by a healthy dose of plastic cups pelting the cage. Haskin seemed to relish the "invading heel" role. He gun-flexed and kiss-blowed for the benefit of the enraged audience.

Finally, two of his corner men managed to peel him down from the wall and nudge him toward the middle of the cage, where a post-fight interviewer stood, gripping the mic and shaking in his loafers.

"Time to vamoose?" Neil asked.

"Like we've never vamoosed before!" Luke replied.

Neil took Tina, his lovely companion, by the hand and brisk-stepped it thru the rapidly emptying VIP section. Luke and Anna followed in lockstep behind them.

Just as the crowd calmed down a bit, the Assassin said something into the mic that inflamed their spirits again. Neil ducked just in time to evade a flying lighter. *Guess cups aren't enough to convey the outrage anymore.*

The four of them reached the arena lobby.

"Everybody in one piece?"

Tina, Luke, and Anna nodded while keeping their heads on a swivel.

"Lemme ring Costa." Neil pressed his cell phone to his ear, but fat chance he could hear anything with the surrounding noise. He signaled to the others to wait for him there and then stepped out.

"Now that we've gorged, do we have it in us to peek under the education hood? Or is that a ridge too far?"

The CGR burped. "Oops!" She finished chewing a cheesy slice and took a sip from her CitrusFuse® can. "Definitely too far for today. Education is a tangled web, woven by a demented spider. On drugs."

"We'll untangle it." The lobbyist picked up a tiny tomato from her slice. "With a little help from our sun-dried friends."

"Seriously, how good are these things? You hit it on the head with this tomato gimmick."

"Apparently, they grow them in the Vacanto region. Special soil. Special oil. Special sun. So much fun." Cynthia noticed a change on the CGR's face. "Or so the legend goes."

"This stays between us." The CGR leaned in, tapping the corner of her mouth with a napkin. "They grow them on Farmer Dale's fields, same as the cheapo brands. Then they juice 'em up with the flavor of the week. Vacanto my butto. They just get a kickback for lending their mystique."

"Everyone's a winner."

"Except these poor little devils." The CGR devoured a bite of the cheesy, tomato-loaded goodness.

Cynthia laughed. "Is there any topic we **can** finish off tonight? So we avoid the same marathon tomorrow?"

"Rookie. During the last ancillary employee benefits round, the top guy locked fifteen of us in a room until we hammered out a deal. We were in there for **eighteen hours!** The lunatic even had the AUIM guarding the door."

Cynthia was aghast. "What about food? Bodily functions?"

"They ordered from Belinda's Baguette Boutique®. And there was a tiny washroom adjoining the room."

"Did anyone try to leg it thru the washroom?"

"Of course—only to find a Ministry shotgun staring back at him."

They pissed themselves laughing.

"Listen up, gang!" Neil called out to the others after getting off the phone with their driver. "He was able to finagle a spot in the owner's zone. No waiting or nuthin. But we only have a short window before the limo turns into a pumpkin."

They stared at him with blank mugs.

"It means 'shake a leg!'" Neil pointed toward the closest exit. "That a way!" The guys took the girls' hands and ran toward the neon-sign-marked door.

They got out of the arena, but Neil doubted they'd make it to the owner's zone in time. "Hang on, guys, let's rethink this." The group stopped just outside of the exit. "At the risk of sounding male-piggish, would you girls mind taking off your heels so you can run faster?"

Anna shook her head. "I already have all the festering blisters I can handle. No thank you."

Her friends were stunned into silence.

"I'm kidding, you fucks. I mean about the blisters, not the shoes. Those stay on."

"Not the shoes, playa. The shoes . . ." Tina was trying to catch her breath. "The shoes are all we have left."

"Stacie and Marjorie[7] over here," Luke jabbed.

Neil raised his cell phone to his ear. "Lemme see if I can summon Costa."

The driver answered the call, but his voice was drowned out by a throng of people spilling out of the arena.

Neil lowered the phone. "Can't hear squat. Let's pick up the pace and we might catch—"

Luke raised his arm and waved past Neil. He turned around and saw what seemed like a mirage—headlights emerging thru a parting sea of people. When he realized it was an ambulance, his shoulders slumped, and he turned back toward Luke. "Thought it was our guy for a second. Way to get my hopes up, buddy."

Luke gave him the old "mouth shut, eyes open" sign and gestured again toward the vehicle. "A Costa by any other name."

Neil squinted at the approaching ambulance and spotted Costa at the wheel, wearing a paramedic's uniform.

As the ambulance rolled past them, Costa jerked his thumb at Neil, who snapped out of his zombie freeze and motioned to the others to form a line behind him.

They walked halfway around the arena before Costa determined the coast was clear and stopped the ambulance. Neil swung open the back door, and the four of them jumped inside. He shut the door

---

7   Stacie Koblenz and Marjorie Whitmore: a comedic duo from the 1930s. In 1938, they became the first all-female act to be shown on Athenian television.

and then banged on the partition. "Cargo safely secured! Make those sirens wail!"

Costa did precisely that, and soon they were watching the arena lights fade into oblivion.

"Agenda for Monday: first draft of the casino scheme, education discussions, and new Muskeg pipeline examination. Sound good?"

The CGR's eyes widened. "You know about the pipeline? I thought it was top secret."

The lobbyist one-eyed her. "Oh, I'm sure everyone who knows about it also knows it's the toppest of secrets. But we might as well take a look at how it could fit into our plans. Meaning, the Yorba Woods Terra Libera government's plans."

The CGR shook her head. "Sounds so weird."

"What does?"

"'Terra Libera government.' All the guy did was cash out the previous viscount.* Now he's head of government. He used to be a hitman."

"Now, that is **definitely** top secret."

The CGR grinned. "To everyone who knows."

"Aside from that, agenda is good?"

"Those three topics are all behemoths, but we'll give it a shot. Over the top, comrades!"

Cynthia laughed, then jotted down a few figures on her notepad. "So it shall be written . . ."

She looked up at the CGR, who held up the next-to-last pizza slice. "So it shall be done."

"Donuts or Nothing®, everybody?" Neil asked the gang. All of them nodded in agreement.

Donuts or Nothing® was a legendary late-night snack joint just outside the downtown core. Whenever the four of them hit the AC nightlife, they would pay a visit to the homely corner caff on Larue Street before continuing to a club or a restaurant.

He pressed the intercom. "Costa, my brother, take us to where the donuts grow."

"Land of the donut it is, sir."

"And thanks again for getting us out of there."

"All in a day's work."

Neil sank deeper in the back seat of the stretch limo. Tina was sitting next to him, and Luke and Anna were in the opposite seat, guzzling mineral water from tiny bottles. All four of them looked drained from the evening's festivities.

It turned out Costa had realized the four of them wouldn't make it to the owner's zone in time, so he palmed a grand to one of his paramedic buddies, who let him take the ambulance for a spin. While Costa was cruising around the arena, the paramedic drove the limo to an agreed-upon spot about fifteen minutes away. Once Costa picked up the group, he drove to the rendezvous point and returned the ambulance.

"One for the ages, eh, gang?" Neil said, trying to boost the troops' morale. "We'll be laughing about it for years to come."

"Next time we do one of **our** things." Tina pointed at herself and Anna. "Winery tour. Cheese tasting. Spa inspection."

"Gallery gazing. Truffle sniffing." Anna smiled, air toasting with her water.

"Just gimme my Caramel Cornucopia," Luke was looking forward to his chalk donut. "While I mourn all those lost zalers."

"Fifty K, right?" That's how much Luke had wagered on Brundell.

"Down the old drain." Luke plucked a fresh bottle from the mini fridge and pressed it against his temple.

"At least you got a good story out of it." Neil scooped up a handful of peanuts and airlifted them into his gob.

"How can you eat those?" Tina asked. "Aren't you thirsty?"

"They're unsalted." Neil shrugged. "Gotta stay on course with my nutritionals. The new condition guy is a real stickler."

Luke grinned. "He's an athlete, don't forget."

"Damn straight." Neil finished off the peanuts and reached for the fridge.

"He's gotta keep that ass of his in top shape coz he's sitting on it ten hours a day," Luke said.

"Feeling better?" Neil twist-opened a peach-flavored Bubbles O' Bliss® and raised the half-liter bottle. "I'm glad. Bottoms up go the bubbles!" He chugged the drink, burped like a pro, then slumped back in the seat. "Deaf leading the blind, I spy a donut sign!"

"He's a poet too," Tina observed.

"Afterwards, Mezzo Dolce®?" Luke wanted to get the vote going now, seeing as such debates tended to rage for hours.

"Won't they be closed by the time we get there?" Anna asked.

"Even if they're open, no way we're getting a decent seat this late," Neal added.

"I'll call Lucio," Luke said. "He'll fit us in."

Tina turned to him. "What about the new Bogaccia downtown?"

Luke's eyes widened in surprise. "There's a second Bogaccia now?"

"Yeah," Neil said. "Third one, I think."

"Bogaccia downtown, eh?" Luke mused.

"While you're mulling, can you also be door opening? Our donut dream has become a reality." Neil pointed to Donuts or Nothing® on his left as the limo pulled up behind a five-deep line of cars.

"Ladies first," Luke proclaimed as he opened the door and stepped out onto the curb.

Once the passengers exited the vehicle, Costa lowered the driver's window. "I'll circle back in about fifteen. Call me if there are any delays or advances."

Neil two-finger saluted, and Costa drove off.

"Would you look at this fucking ant line," Luke murmured as the four of them took their place at the rear.

"Chin up, dawg." Neil fist-bumped his buddy's shoulder. "The staff here are ninjas. We'll have you stuck in a donut in no time."

"Stuck in a donut? Like in the hole?"

"Perfect spot!"

The gang howled with laughter. Just as Luke was about to add a pun into the mix, a fireball engulfed the street.

4 Ruin

The small room was suspended in tense silence, every eye around the table glued to the cards in Patton Battaglia's hand.

The White Wizard was sitting across from him, staring daggers and sweating bullets.

They were the last two men standing in a twelve-hour no-holds-barred Ring of Ruin[8] mega session. The pot had ballooned to over nine million zalers. Once Battaglia flipped 'em over, there'd be only one winner, taking home the whole pile.

Battaglia took a swig of his brandy sour, cracked his neck, and placed the first card on the table.

Queen of hearts.

He took one last look at his hand, glanced at the other men at the table, then spread out the rest of his cards.

Six of hearts, six of clubs, six of spades, six of diamonds.

The room gasped. The White Wizard sank in his chair.

Battaglia rose from his seat, closed his eyes, and raised his arms.

"**Momma, can you see me now?!**"

The other players smattered a couple of claps. The winner extended his hand to the runner-up. "Apologies for the outburst,

---

8   Ring of Ruin: a high-risk, high-reward card game of attrition in which participants who start with small amounts can win big and vice versa. Currently enjoying a surge in popularity on the underground circuit.

Your Exaltedness. But you don't retire from law enforcement as a millionaire every day."

The White Wizard shook Battaglia's hand, his own hand limp. "Glad I could help."

The Wizard got out of his chair and wobble-walked into the kitchenette. He opened the faucet and let the cold water run. Once it was properly ice cold, he filled an empty juice canister to the brim and took a few gulps. Then he closed the canister and pressed it against his heart, trying to get a rapid cooldown going.

All the players had left the table and were now standing in a semicircle around the winner, firing off questions.

"How did you know I was bluffing the rank?"

"When I folded, did you figure Larry would go next?"

"Was I telegraphing my hands?"

"Tell me, should I have pressed the issue harder when I had you on the ropes?"

"Did you knowingly sic the Wizard on me in hour eight?"

Battaglia's eyes sparkled with joy as he fielded every ball thrown at him. But he also looked drained, which reminded the Wizard of his own level of exhaustion now that his nerves had come down from their multi-hour high-wire act.

He opened the small door that led into the hardware store's loading area. The owner let them use one of the back rooms against a cut of the house's take. Not that they needed to worry about the cops busting up the game. It was merely a convenient central location for all the players, plus there was no nosey hotel staff to shoo away.

Still holding the canister to his chest, the Wizard took a few steps into the loading zone. As he stood there in the dark, cooling down, he noticed a pair of cranes shimmering with a high-tech gleam. He strained his eyes at a big red ACHTUNG sign, followed by text that he was unable to decipher from where he stood.

That got him thinking. One surge of courage. One press of a button. One less Wizard.

"Goodbye, cruel world?"

The White Wizard jumped at the voice behind him and spun around.

"Madonna santissima, Kerry, you sure know how to make an entrance!"

Kerry Douglas grinned from one ear to the other. "But you **were** thinking about it, weren't you? Eh? Confess to old Uncle Kerry, o whitest of all wizards."

"Here I am, trying to soothe me dicky ticker, when the Crowbar decides to wrench it outta my chest."

"The Crowbar would never do such a dastardly deed. Not to the Wizard, anyway."

"Much comfort." The Wizard pulled a bee swallow.

Kerry pointed to the canister. "Is it working?"

"The water? Yeah, my body does seem to be cooling down."

"That was a heck of a ride back there. Quite the roller coaster."

"Wish I'd come out on top, is all."

Kerry shrugged. "There's always next week."

The runner-up said nothing.

"Or the week after that."

More silence.

"Or the week after that?"

The Wizard glum-smiled and shook his head. "Nah. Not next week, not next month. Not next ever."

Kerry's eyebrows furrowed with concern. "What's wrong?"

"The White Wizard is now. . . the Skint Lizard."

Crowbar took a step closer and put his arm on the Wizard's shoulder. "The fuck you talkinbout? You own the biggest dental franchise in the goddamn **country!** Skint?! After one bad bounce?"

The Wizard's eyebrows shot up. "'Bad bounce?' Mister Crowbar calls losing seven million zalers a bad bounce? Yeah, now that's a bad bounce and a bloody half." He squeezed the canister a bit harder, trying to find a still-cold spot of water.

"Are you at zero cash after the loss, or are you in a hole?"

"Hole. Big one."

Kerry's mug grew darker. The Wizard kept mum, so Kerry nudged him. "Might as well tell me now, Wiz. No secrets between friends."

"Five . . . five mil." The dentist looked down at his shoes.

"Five? I still don't get it."

"Two ex-wives, kids in best schools, baby mama hush money, seven cars, one yacht, four chefs—one per house—world's ninth-largest AC Sentinels® memorabilia collection, private jet, private golf course—as in, only me and my buddies use it and no one else—second baby mama hush money, wine cellar the size of Farmer Dale's farm, a fiancée whose idea of foreplay is fist fucking my wallet, a private—"

Kerry raised his hand. "Don't tell me—zoo?"

The Wizard frowned. "Why would I want **that?**"

"No reason." Kerry put his arm around the dentist and walked him back into the room. "We'll figure out a payment plan. You sure you can't, like, sell more franchises or something?"

"Soft market."

"Isn't it always?"

"Same as last week! This fuckin' Collins guy, is he naturally slow, or is he taking lessons?"

WUWI superstar Jimmy Lorenz was in the zone, sharing his chicken wings with the room and his wisdom with the world.

"He's tender. His monthly cycle just started again," Buddy One chimed in.

"Eeeew!" Buddy Three protested.

"Gross," Buddy Two agreed.

"Nearly lost a perfectly fine chicken wing." Buddy Five re-dunked the wing in Feuer & Flamme® hot pepper sauce. "OK, back in business." He gulped the piece down and sent a slosh of CherryBlast® Lime down his gullet behind it. "I feel a mega burp coming."

Jimmy signaled to Buddy One. They both got up and went to the bedroom, safe from the cameras.

"**Burrrrp!** There it is."

"Oh, and **I'm** the gross one?" Buddy One called out to the living room before he and Jimmy entered the bedroom and switched off their mics.

"What the hell was **that?!**" Jimmy glared at his lieutenant.

"The cycle thing? No good?"

"Did you sleep thru the meeting again? We're trying to grow the audience over here. You gotta keep it clean, dawg."

Buddy One sighed. "I know. I hear you." He rubbed his neck. "I worry that if I pull a muzzler, I won't be funny no more."

"When were you ever funny?"

Buddy One snort-laughed. "Fuck you too."

Jimmy smiled. "We got it made in the shade here. A couple of knuckleheads like us won't get another gig like this in ten lifetimes. You know that."

"True that. I don't take this shit for granted."

Jimmy nodded. "Good boy. Now let's get back in there before they start thinking we're whacking each other off."

"Let me introduce Toni 'Titbuster' Gomez." Kerry waved Toni over. "But you can call him Buster."

They were standing in the hardware store's employee parking lot, next to the White Wizard's car.

The Wizard shook Toni's hand. "Mind if I ask how you got that nickname?"

"My name is Antonio." Toni's hammerhead mug remained grim.

"No, I meant the other, um, the other name, Tit, um, Titb . . ." The Wizard trailed off.

"Chicks dig the long pole."

The Wizard eye-darted between Kerry and Toni for a few awkward ticks before all three of them burst into laughter.

"Buster will be your account manager. He'll make sure the payment plan is adhered to."

"How does it work? I call him once a week or . . ."

"No need to call. Buster will be right next to you, twenty-four/seven."

The White Wizard was taken aback, but he didn't protest.

"You got everything, Buster? Your gear, your toiletries, and all that?" Crowbar asked.

"Sure. I keep a bag in the car."

"Total pro." Kerry head-pointed at Buster while looking at the Wizard.

The back door burst open, and out hustled Patton Battaglia, his winter coat in hand.

"There he is!" Kerry said. "A detective and a gentleman."

"Rarely a gentleman, and a dec not for long." Battaglia grinned as he headed for his car.

"What's the rush? I thought money never runs."

"All I got is plastic chips. When **am** I getting the do-re-mi, by the way?"

"Monday," Kerry assured him. "Twelve o'clock on the dot."

"Somebody pinch me."

"I can make a call," Buster offered.

"Nah, gotta run." Battaglia laughed. "Shit went down downtown."

"What happened?" the Wizard asked, pretending to care.

"Possible terror sitch."

As Crowbar, Buster, and Wizard stared at him with stunned mugs, Battaglia got into his unmarked sedan, waved, and then peeled out.

"Never a dull one." Kerry shook the other men's hands and went back inside. The Wizard got into his car and drove off, Buster following.

Jimmy Lorenz was eye-scanning data for the session that had just ended. It was a big college pixkin clash, and they had done well. Twelve hundred new subscribers and eight thousand affiliate purchases. A 20 percent engagement bump and a whopping fifty thousand Attaboy™ tokens, which translated to about seven thousand zalers.

"WUWI" stood for "Watch Us Watch It." Punters paid to watch an online stream of Jimmy and the gang watching sports events at Jimmy's house. The cameras were set up to capture feeds from the living room, the kitchen, the den (which featured a display of jerseys, pixkins, sticks, bobbleheads, helmets, pucks, die-cast monster trucks, bats, and foam fingers), and the garage, where a custom-built AC Hogs®-branded mini pool table stood. Viewers could switch between the feeds at any time. Naturally, most of the action took place in the living room, where an eighty-inch screen beamed with pride.

As with many life-changing inventions, this form of entertainment was discovered by accident. Jimmy and his twin brother, Tommy, were online gaming one night but got tired and, with their mics unmuted, started watching an ACF® show instead. Their banter caught the attention of other zockers, and soon more people were listening to them than playing the game. Tommy was the first one to see the potential, deciding to offer it as a service and see what happened.

What happened was a bonanza. Their format took off and turned into a moneymaker within six months. One year later, Jimmy quit his warehouse manager job and went pro. Tommy had no job to quit, but he still had dreams of street thuggery to pursue.

Once his brother dropped out, Jimmy added his most suitable friends to the mix—some behind the camera and some in front of it. The on-air crew consisted of Jimmy and the Four Buddies, with occasional guest appearances by other friends and family. Although many a C-list dweller expressed interest in dropping a floater, WUWI so far shunned celebs for fear of authenticity-breaking. They chose to keep streaming from Jimmy's house for the same reason, even though they could easily afford to gimmick a soundstage to look exactly like the rooms in the house. They figured the fans would find out instantly and unleash a backlash of epic proportions. WUWI regularly cracked the national top ten, eclipsed only by streams in which girls either tried clothes on or took clothes off. You don't mess with a cash cow like that just coz your privacy is hurting.

Jimmy's Earwig® hummed—yet another post-show message. He glanced at the screen and, just as expected, there was a note from management concerning Buddy One's boneheaded comment. He typed "already addressed, won't re-happen" and clicked "send."

For the next ten minutes, he was going over the show's highlights and lowlights—what could be improved, what should be avoided. He made a point of giving the bare minimum of guidance to the Buddies. If their behavior felt coached, WUWI's appeal would go to the dogs. He settled on three details to point out to the gang. Two concerned tech issues (camera angles and sound), and one had to do with fugazi stats that Buddy Three had tried to peddle as facts.

That oughta do it for tonight. Jimmy stretched, yawned, downed the last of his product-placed Mocha Muchachos® Inflagrante™, squashed the can, missed the waste basket, then got up from the chair, slam-dunked the can, and shuffled off to his bedroom.

On his way there, he flicked off lights. *Note to self: ask management about a kill switch for all these frickin' lights.* Just as he reached the bedroom door and was about to put his Earwig® on full mute, the gizmo hummed again.

The message made him frown in puzzlement. He clicked "call."

"Jimmy? Thanks for getting back."

"Um . . . sure thing, Mister Malanga." Vincent Malanga Sr. owned a joint on Levski Point. Last Jimmy heard, the place was enjoying a second spring due to the recent gentrification. Tommy and Vinnie Jr. were bosom buds. "How's the remodeling going?"

"The remodeling? Oh, the rooftop patio. Smooth as butter, thanks for asking."

"Glad to hear. Holla if you need a helping hand, I know a few guys, real reliable."

"I will. Erm . . . "

"Is something wrong? Are you looking for Junior? Haven't seen him today."

Vinnie Sr. sighed. "Are you sitting down?"

5 Horizon

"Farmer" Dale Hofstetter stopped his Corn Crusher® 5200X in front of Silo 7.

"Now we'll see what's really going on."

"Think it's a bum airbag?" Randy Hendricks, his son-in-law, asked.

"My money's on bridging. We've seen it before with this one."

"Cleaning these old bastards? A living hell."

"Don't I know it."

The two men exited the farm vehicle and walked over to the silo. The day was mild with a sunny sky and just a hint of wind. If only farming was that easy every day.

Farmer Dale opened the door and stepped into the crawlspace that contained the control console. After making sure all the switches were off and the unloader safety was on, he pointed to the filters ahead. "Spot me!"

"You sure? Shouldn't I go first?"

"Age before beauty."

Randy chortled. "You're the boss."

"Though not for long, maybe."

"Not **that** again. They just want an itty-bitty piece. And you're the sole shot caller."

"Don't I know it." Farmer Dale winked and then made his way along the treacherous ladder that led to the air filters.

"All good up there?" Randy's voice crackled thru the Earwig® that hung on Dale's lapel. "I'll lose the visual after the next rung. For about thirty ticks."

"Thirty? Three zero?"

"Yeah."

"Copy that, Delta Zebra. All good so far."

"Cut the jokes, Turbo Grampa. You lose your focus and we'll be scraping you off the floor with a spoon."

"A spoon of Farmer Dale's®. Literally!"

"Focus, good sir!"

"Just keep shining that flashlight."

Hugo Jimenez straightened his tie and pulled up his pants. He mulled tightening his belt one notch more but decided to leave it for the moment. His newly discovered active lifestyle had left him in between notches. *Better hit that treadmill harder if I wanna reach the next belt hole.*

As he waited for Sigma to reappear, his eye kept darting toward the AUIM statue in the lobby. Esteban was right; the uniform was a splendor to behold.* Somehow, the lobby seemed the perfect spot for it.

Just as Hugo glanced at his watch, Sigma came back down the stairs. "Deepest apologies for the delay, Mr. Jimenez. The viscount will see you now."

Hugo jolted. "Damn, it sounds good to hear that! 'The viscount will see you now.' I felt a surge just now." He picked up his briefcase. "But no need to bow, Sigma. We're all trench veterans here."

"Thank you, sir. But as I'm sure you know . . . viscount's orders."

"Lead on." Hugo palm-pointed upstairs, but Sigma nixed it.

"He's in his air chamber."

The lawyer's mug was awash in puzzlement. Sigma smirked. "This way."

"Randy, my boy! Where's that spotlight?"

"Nix the holla, Farmer Dale. I'm picking you up crystally on the comm."

"It's getting darker by the second up here."

"As it should. But you'll be hitting the flash in about five meters. If you look up, maybe you can already see a bit of it."

"I **am** looking up. The hell you think—roger, I see a sparkle." Farmer Dale continued the strenuous ascent.

"I did offer to go in your stead."

"How mighty noble."

"Well, I did!"

"Nix the holla. Coming up on the trickiest part here."

"Easy does it."

"Are these the OceanFlood® 60s or 70s?"

"Which color are they?"

"Darker than a witch cat's bumhole up in here."

"We should know this."

"And yet we don't."

"Hang on." Randy pulled a fiddler on his cell phone. "No signal."

"I can hear you fine."

"Nah, I meant on my cell. Was gonna interweb it regarding the filter."

"Tell you what. Hit the panel, and throw the security switch back off. Give it five ticks and then switch it back on. Do that twice."

"You sure, Dale? Them cracklers know no master. If they blow, **we** blow."

"Untwist those tangled undies this instant, lieutenant! They're security switches, not bomb wires. Ghosts and goblins over here."

"Alright," Randy murmured, then did as instructed.

A minute later, Farmer Dale's voice came back on the comm. "It ain't the filters. They're breathing just fine."

"Damn it to hell. All this huffin for nuffin."

"Well, at least we crossed it off the old list. Up next, the jaws of death."

"At least the weather's good."

"Flashlight!"

Sigma stopped in front of a door in the opposite wing from where the viscount's office was. "Just keep walking until you see him."

Hugo twitched. "Okay."

Sigma opened the door, and the lawyer stepped in.

He was hit by flowery scents and misty air. The room was dark and humid. Wooden walls, stone floors. *The fuck is this, a sauna?* He was told to keep walking, so he did.

As he made his way across the slippery floor in his dress shoes, a voice came floating thru the mist. "What is it that you seek, baldheaded pilgrim? Truth, enlightenment? Justice, perhaps? If so, you came to the wrong place, for you will find none of them here. All we have is pretzels."

Hugo belly-laughed. "Don't do this to me, Esteban old chap, unless you want to see me kertwang my ass on these stones. Moist floor and dress shoes? Recipe for destruction."

"Come closer, tired traveler. Let the viscount envelop you in his light."

Hugo followed the sound of the voice and finally set his eyes on the man he had come to see, sitting in what seemed like a yoga pose. "Esteban Estez Junior. Mister Estez. Don Esteban. The viscount of Yorba Woods. The Right Honorable. The Guarantor of the Autonomy. The Protector of the Helpless. The Bezwinger of the Wicked. What am I forgetting?"

"I hope not coffee."

"To wash down the pretzels?" Hugo smirked. "Nah, I didn't bring any."

"Good thing we have a gallon of it sitting over there." With his eyes still closed, Esteban head-pointed to a table with snacks and an espresso machine off to the side.

"Are you . . . um . . . doing yoga or . . ."

"Never thought you'd see the day, eh? It helps with decluttering." The viscount tapped his temple.

"If you grow a ponytail, I'm out."

Both men laughed for a solid minute.

"Jaws of death, open!"

Nothing happened.

"Jaws of the deathly kind, I command you to open!"

Still zilch.

"O ye jaws of the deadliest persuasion, I endeavor you to—"

"Knock it off." Farmer Dale cut down Randy's theatricals as he sank further down the grain pile. They were trying to reach the silo's unloading chute, known lovingly among maintenance folk as the jaws of death. One wrong move and a gruesome (albeit quick) death awaited. "Lemme see if I can unhatch it with my magic finger."

"'Unhatch,' sir?"

"Unlatch the hatch. Equals unhatch. I'm putting words together for devastating effect. Or so I invainly hoped."

"'Invainly.' Like in vain. Coz I didn't compute it."

"Look at that big-ass brain go!"

"Dale, I'm givin' it two more minutes. If you can't unhatch it, we gotta split and send in the hydraulic boys."

Silence.

"Dale? Dale!"

"Still alive. Though barely. A big ol' air pocket almost got me."

"You need to get your bony ol' butt back here now! Sir."

"True words of precious wisdom. Out I go."

"How is Castle Jimenez coming along?"

"Slow and unsteady. Every time I think it's done, the missus decides to add another wing."

Esteban grinned. "Tell me about it. I mostly use this room to hide from the viscountess's railings against the handyman unions."

"You allow those?"

"Age-old tradition in these parts. Buying the people's affection."

"The viscount paint is still fresh. Treading lightly?"

"Yes, but not for too long." Esteban flowed into a new yoga pose. "The people need to know there's a new hand twirling the six shooter. A strong, bulging, thick-veined, fast-drawing, gnarly, battle-scarred hand. No more cobweb-covered cuddly passive ways of old."

"Passivity." Hugo snorked. "If there's one thing I hate."

"We'll turn this place onto its sleepy head. They'll be calling it 'the astonishing turnaround.' Or something. The media, that is."

"Cynthia is working her magic, by the way. But no definitive progress yet."

"I'm not worried about Cynthia." Esteban turned on his side and stretched his left leg. "Cynthia will do just fine. Our ferocious burrower. Our velvet glove."

"Our mighty megamole."

"I told you we needed a female touch on the case. Still waters. Men are no good at burrowing. They get distracted by boobs halfway thru."

"Whereas women have boob access at all times."

"Thereby nixing the need to go boob hunting."

"Ain't nature grand?"

Slam! Farmer Dale shut the Corn Crusher® 5200X door and sat back in the shotgun seat.

"Bridging, eh?" He exhaled a long breath and squinted at Randy in the driver's seat. "We gotta switch over to the new tubes. Meaning, all the way. The entire storage, not just around the core. Can't keep hangin' on like a zombie on a titty."

"We need to protect these fields too." Randy pointed to the prairie around the silo.

Dale shrugged. "Is it still worth it?"

"Good thing I quit the bottle or there'd be one big sudsy mess on this here windshield. **Farmer Dale?** Farmer Dale of Farmer Dale's® sees no point no more? Farmer Dale who built the goddamn prairie with his own two knobby hands? Farmer Dale whose blood feeds the soil and makes the veggies grow? Hey, who's this imposter sitting next to me in this here farm mobile?"

"You're a good egg, son-in-law number five. Even though you're still confused about how prairies work."

They laughed as Randy started the corn-fueled engine and directed the vehicle onto the gravel path leading toward the main road.

"I tell ya, it ain't like it used to be. The crop game. It was always a backbreaker but not like it is now. The goddamn razor's edge tickling our nuts every month."

"Month in, month out," Randy agreed, nodding. "But the Dale Battalion perseveres. Onward and upward!"

"Oh, we're in the army too? Firefightin' ain't enough?"

"Ha! Have you given any further spins to the thought of hangin' up the big hose?"

"I ain't even touching that one. Too easy. Gimme something hard."

"That's what **she** said. Way too easy."

"The big hose shall remain firmly in these here knobby, prairie-building hands. Those fires gotta find a way past the old Dusty Dale if they wanna gobble up these here lands." Dale pointed at the fields wind-bowing around them.

"Oh yeah? Like last time? Remember Rural 99?"

"Don't go askin' like you ain't graspin'. Nearly lost my damn license to live. Natch I remember."

"And still you wanna keep playing the superhero. Dusty Dale, the Flame Retard."

"Sure hope you meant to say 'Retardant.'"

"You know of any other industry leaders risking their bacon in volunteer firefights?"

"I don't give a rat's hairy hind for what other industry leaders are doing or ain't doing. I've always gone my own way. The Farmer Dale's® way. Registered trademark and all."

"The time has come for younger folk to stick their necks out."

"If I ain't the guy on the logo, all the schemes are a no go."

"Two-minute warning." Esteban was wrapping up his session. "Go on, grab some java."

Hugo went over to the table and quick-scanned the coffee pod bowl. A dark roast flavor smiled at him. He took out the pod, dropped it into the KaffaCasa® ForzaPressa™, and hit the red button.

"Boom! Four seconds." He picked up the cup and turned back to Esteban. "Y'know, we're having one of these installed on every floor of Castle Jimenez."

"Never run out."

"A four-tic cuppa joe, always within reach."

"Are you getting a deal on the machines?"

"Due to volume? Nah. Bastards know their brand's allure and are wielding it with wicked glee."

"Speaking of brand building, have you tried the pretzels?"

"Pretzels?" Hugo turned toward the snack table. "Soft and sexy?"

"See for yourself."

The lawyer reached for a pretzel and then spotted the name and logo on the box. "Get It Twisted™?! From the prison bust out?"

"It went viral. Everybody and their mother wants a taste of infamy."

"What's wrong with us?" Hugo bit into a pretzel.

"Us Athenians? Nothing. We're dreamers."

"You see yourself as Athenian? Not Kalimban?"

"Both." Esteban grimaced as he stretched into his routine's final position. "But I'm the viscount of Yorba Woods first. Soaring above the scourge of tribalism."

"Almost angelic."

"They raised the offer. Twenty percent."

"Magma did?"

Dale nodded. "Threatening with imports and alternative supply lines in case we keep logjammin'."

"You know how empty that threat is? If you dried out all the oceans, that's how empty."

"I dunno, Randy old boy. Two years, I'd say it'd take 'em."

"Long enough for the damn country to starve."

"Would they care?"

"Riddle me this, father-in-law number one: who'll be buying their miracle potion if everyone is stone dead?"

"Point taken. Still, it's a whole heap o' happy paper."

"What would you do with it? If you had all that do-re-mi?"

Dale's eyes got googly. "I'd sail, Randy, me son. Sail away into the blue yonder. Just me and Mother Maci. No more shoveling mule shit for this here farmhand."

"My ears must be clogged with said mule shit coz I could swear you just said you'd up and turn your behind on your boy Randy here and the other thirty-nine hungry mouths needin' feedin'."

"I ain't sayin' forever! Not like I'd go pullin' a Zombie Sailor for all eternity. A year. Maybe two. Until the fond heart grows . . . until the fondness in your heart . . . in **my** heart—how does it go again?"

"Never you mind about no one's heart, Farmer Dale, coz you just done shattered mine. Took a big-ass baseball bat and clubbed the poor ol' ticker into a mulchy pulp. Just look at it, lying there non-beating on the mangy floor. You can't even tell it was once a human heart capable of giftin' love."

Dale put his hand on Randy's shoulder. "You'd be in charge while I'm gone. Whip the brood into shape."

Randy glanced at him and then refocused on the road. "What about Mother Maci, eh? No way in hell she'd follow you into your fond yonder."

Dale wrist-flicked. "You asked me what I would do with a cash injection. So that's what I would do. Guess I should've said what I'd **like** to do if my hands were untied. Coz you're right; Mother Maci is a tough stone to turn."

"Gave birth to eight giant babies, some of them mid-harvest. Solid bloody rock."

"Dare to dream."

"I see you got one of the dark roasts. I'm feeling minty." Having finished his morning meditation, Esteban joined Hugo at the snack table.

After ForzaPressa™ did its four-second turbo whirr, the viscount took the cup filled with Minty Wintry™ and downed it. "Hoowee! Who knew this flavor would be what my heart desired today? Usually, I don't like mint in my java."

"Maybe it's the exercise. How long have you been yoging it up?"

"Not long. I wanna say two months. Since around the time we started hounding Lin. I wanna be my most calm and collected self for the big day."

Hugo paused. "Please tell me you're joking."

Esteban laughed. "I just wanted to see your mug." He fingerjabbed the lawyer in the ribs. "Worried that old Esteban has gone over to the soft side, eh? Sweating to harp music and whoring for the cameras?"

"The thought never crossed my mind." Hugo munched the last of his pretzel.

"How come there's no baked goodness in **my** hand?" The viscount turned around and took out a sour cream-flavored pretzel from one of the Get It Twisted™ boxes. "Gnam!"

"They have a store here? In Yorba?"

"No." Esteban shook his head. "Not yet anyway. I had these flown in this morning from Muskeg."

"How come they're still fresh and fantabulous?"

"They arrived frozen. My guys heated 'em up."

The lawyer fluttered his shirt. "Speaking of heat, is His Excellency not warm?"

"Feeling despair due to hot air?" Esteban said between bites. "One touch of a button and all will be fair." He walked over to a small panel on the wall and clicked it. Within ten ticks the room was awash in coolness.

"How . . . what is this devilry?"

"You didn't see the latest issue? Tsk, tsk. You need to start putting those billions* to better use."

"Issue? Of what, DiamondBlack®?"

"DiamondBlack®, he says. There's at least two higher catalogs."

"Two? I had no idea. And I'm supposed to know everything."

"They're invite only. I think they only go out to official double-digit billionaires. I know you've got around ten, but you're keeping it under the radar."

"Off the books and away from crooks."

"You can have my copy."

"No! I'll be tempted, and I can't afford it—yet. But good to know."

"See? There's always a higher rainbow." Esteban walked back to the table. "Speaking of which, ready to join me on a trip tomorrow?"

"Where are we going?"

The viscount bit off a piece of pretzel. "Into the fires of hell."

6 Roach

"Today, Magma mourns the loss of one of its favorite sons. Luke O'Reilly, a member of the RED ORE® O'Reilly family, was killed last night in a horrific incident in downtown Athenia City. A flamethrower-wielding assailant left devastation in his wake as he opened fire in front of a busy late-night snack shop on Larue Street. Footage from the store's security camera—the store appears to have been at least a partial target—shows the masked attacker emerging from an alley and spraying the area in front of the store with flames. The attack lasted for about thirty seconds, at which point the assailant disappeared into the alley from which he came. Five victims were left lying on the ground, with fellow patrons and bystanders coming to their aid in a frantic scene."

Lin Wesley took a moment.

"We will now show the security camera footage, in hopes that the public might recognize the attacker or notice any other pertinent details. Please be warned: these images are extremely disturbing. Any viewers who wish to make use of the Blackout™ button on their remote controls should do so now and then press the button again after sixty seconds. Thank you."

She scanned the mugs of the crew in the studio. Industry veterans to a person, yet all of them wore expressions of stunned bewilderment. This wasn't a foreign war or a distant quake. It was a flamethrower attack in downtown AC. This was new.

"And we're back," she said sixty seconds later. "Next up, we'll hear from the lead investigator, AC Metro's Patton Battaglia. Our reporters spoke to him earlier today at the precinct."

The feed switched to a pair of decs, referred to by the infographic as Patton Battaglia and Benji Gutierrez, pressed against a wall by a platoon of mics.

Lin glanced at the digits on her desk. The cop segment would be followed by an ad block. Time to check her Earwig® for the latest Rusty rub.

"Where is he? Where is he, so I can wring his fucking neck once and for all?"

"I don't know, Jimmy, I swear. He's gone to ground."

Jimmy Lorenz and Vincent "Lucky" Malanga Sr. were grilling Vincent "Lucky" Malanga Jr. on the whereabouts of Tommy Lorenz.

"Don't you know all his places? Secret, non-secret, mid-secret . . ."

"Sure, Pops, but he ain't gonna go to one of those. Not now. Not after this."

Lucky Senior was sitting next to Junior on the living room couch of their Levski Point house. Jimmy was pacing back and forth in front of them.

"Do you know what area?" Jimmy asked. "Like, the neighborhood at least? Levski? Bronson somewhere?"

Lucky Junior racked his brain. "One part of me says Bronson. He wouldn't be foolish enough to come back to Levski, y' know? But then another part of me says maybe he would, on account of nobody expecting it."

Jimmy shot Junior a look of exasperation and continued pacing.

"Hey, what about food? Liquids? You think he would've stashed it somewhere beforehand? Hidden lair-type thing."

"I dunno, Pops. I just . . . you know how he is. Sometimes he plans things out. Other times he acts ass over head. Jimmy knows. Obviously."

"Yeah, I know how he gets. My imbecilic twin of a brother."

"Don't you two have a special bond? ESP or something? I ain't being a wise ass."

Jimmy slowed his pacing. "There's a bond. I can feel him in my bones sometimes. But if you're asking whether I can sense where he is right now, it ain't like that. If I knew where the momo was, I'd have beelined there as soon as Senior gave me the news."

"**Leo!**"

Here we go again.

"Those teal gloves, have you seen them? Don't tell me I left them in the car [inaudible]."

Leo went thru the standard routine of turning on his back, blinking, glancing at the nightstand clock, closing his eyes again, trying to catch a few more precious minutes of shut-eye—all the while trying to decipher Beli's verbal whirls.

"Pretty sure I saw them in the garage." *Can she hear me?* "When we came back last night."

"Garage?! Since when do we keep gloves in the garage? What about the poor cars, eh? Where will **they** sleep?"

Leo mock applauded. "Tres amusant, ma cherie."

"Damn straight." Beli went downstairs, presumably expanding her glove-hunting radius.

Leo burped and then got out of bed. He headed for the bathroom but then stopped dead in his tracks as a familiar melody rang out across the room. He whipped around and saw that his other cell phone was ringing. Only Neil Zorich knew the number. Leo hadn't spoken to him in a year.

With a vibe of rising dread, he picked up the phone. "Hello?"

"Who's the handsomest boy in all of pretzeldom?"

"Um . . . me, I guess?"

"Such modesty. Flex those pythons."

"Um . . . you can see me?"

"Just messing with ya."

"Oh! I see."

"Long time no squawk."

"Yes . . . erm . . . way too long, I'd say. Y'know, I woulda called, but I always feel like I'm imposing with you guys."

"What guys?"

"The Zoriches."

"Nonsense. You're off the blacklist and back in our good graces.* Give us a hug."

"I'll hug the phone. How's that?"

Neil laughed. "Have you seen the news?"

"No, I just got up. What happened? Not those bloody bombers again."

"No. Well . . . in a way. I'll let you get to it. Check out Channel 5®. Any channel, really. It's all over the place. Call you in a bit."

"We're back with you here at Channel 5® as we continue our extended coverage of the Athenia City flame attack. Our reporter, Flip Johnson, is at the scene with the latest. Flip, how would you describe the mood around the attack site?"

"Lin, if I had to use one word, it would be 'eerie.' Normally, this intersection is a hub of activity, but right now the only people present are law enforcement personnel. As you can see behind me, they've screened off the area in front of the Donuts or Nothing® shop as they collect evidence."

"Flip, is there any word on how it was possible for this attacker to slip away unnoticed with so many people around?"

Flip frowned and pressed his palm against his ear. "Lin, I lost you there for a second. Did you say how come no one noticed a masked person with a flamethrower?"

Lin nodded. "Yes."

Flip turned and pointed to a scaffolding next to the donut shop. "You see this building over there? It's part of a 'round-the-clock construction site that stretches all the way to the other side of Larue Street, some five blocks. What we've learned so far is that several people saw the man but assumed he was part of the work crew. Apparently, he was even wearing a safety helmet. Some witness accounts mention him also wearing an owl mask, but that's yet to be confirmed."

"Any news on his getaway route?"

"The police haven't stated anything publicly. Our sources tell us there are indications he might have had an accomplice, possibly in the form of a getaway driver."

Jimmy raised his eyebrows at Lucky Junior. "So, getaway driver to the stars. Where did you drive him?"

"**Nowhere.** That's the point. I was sitting there, thinking, 'What the hell am I doing here?! If he goes ahead with it, I'll be considered an accessory.' So, I left the keys in the van and hopped on a subway home. He can drive himself, the goddamn lunatic."

"Do you know if he got back to the van?"

"No clue."

Jimmy had stopped pacing and planted himself in front of the couch, pumping Junior for info. Lucky Senior was upstairs, getting dressed for the day.

"Why the fuck did you let him go? Why didn't you stop him?"

"I didn't think he'd go thru with it! You know how many times he's come to me with plans from hell, and I shot them down? And even when I didn't, he'd chicken out or modify them to the point of being harmless."

"Well, he didn't modify this one! This one was one spectacularly enormous disaster from start to finish!"

"I ain't arguing. But how can I help? I never ever gave one iota of info to the cops, never in me bloody life. You ask anybody, I'm a mute statue. But in this case, I'll squeal if you want me to. Just say the word. I mean, attacking civvies? Burning those poor bastards? Tommy broke the code."

"The code? The code of the streets? Yeah, no shit he broke it. Broke it, sat on it and unloaded his burrito lunch all over it."

"I can smell the nacho cheese from here. And the charred corpses."

"How many dead?"

"Let's find out." Lucky Junior reached for the remote and unmuted the box.

"What. In the actual. Fuck?" Leo plumped onto the bed as he gazed at his bedroom box, his mouth hanging open. "I'm losfer words. And how often does that happen?"

"A monk you are not, mon ami," Neil replied.

"How . . . how did you guys wind up at that spot?"

"We caught the fight. Haskin—Brundell. Crowd got unruly after their boy got dropped. Our driver got us outta there in a frickin' ambulance."

"Whoa. He greased the paramedics?"

"Yep."

"Some night."

"Unrepeatable."

"Let's hope so, eh? How did you survive?"

"Out of the corner of my eye, I saw a flash of fire. Autopilot kicked in—I grabbed the two girls and pushed them to the ground. I laid on top of them until the ordeal was over."

"Were you hurt?"

"Singed and dazed. The girls too, minor stuff. But of course . . ."

"The O'Reilly dude."

"It's a blur, but I think he was the first one to get caught by the flames. No chance to blink, let alone get out of the way."

"Did you see the footage on TV?"

"Not of the actual attack. Still too raw."

Leo sighed. "I don't . . . I don't know what to say."

"Tell ya what. The circus will be hitting Stavenage next week. Come see me at the track, cheer me up."

"Um . . . sure. What time and day?"

"The race is on Saturday night. Teams will start arriving late Tuesday. I'm thinking Wednesday noonish."

"I'll be there."

"We'll be racing glow-in-the-dark paint schemes. It'll be a sight to behold."

"I can feel the seizure **already.**"

"Trying to bait me into laughter? I'm mourning a BFF here."

"Sorry, Neal. I don't know what came over me."

"Make it up by bringing a haul of pretzels with you. Stavenage Santa-style."

"Sure thing. I'll use our Baker Bunker Bag™. They'll be as good as fresh."

"You can't stop progress."

"Lin, we've just learned that the four people wounded in the attack have been upgraded to 'stable' or higher as they receive care at a nearby shpitz. Luke O'Reilly remains the only casualty of this senseless act."

"Thank you, Flip. We'll be checking back with you later in the evening."

"Thanks, Lin."

The anchorwoman addressed the audience. "This camera angle change brought to you by Feed the Feast®. Get ten zalers off your starter kit order when you use code CHAN5. Feed the Feast®—**now** you're cookin'. Up next, sports and weather. And **I** will see you for the nine o'clock news. This is Lin Wesley. Stay safe, and keep your eye on Channel 5®."

She held the smile for five ticks and then pretend-shuffled the papers in front of her. Once the "all clear" flashed on her desk screen, she rolled her chair back and made a beeline for her office.

"Baby Lin!"

Her manager's voice startled her as she rounded a corner.

"Mother of Gawd, Rusty, what's with the ambush in the bush cobblers?"

Rusty Blevins gave her an innocent look. "You responded to my message. I thought you read it."

"I did. Didn't you say you'd meet me in my office?"

"I didn't mean **literally.** Entering your office before you get there? I wouldn't dream of it."

"See how I'm smirking knowingly?"

Rusty gave it two thumbs up. "That is some primo smirking of the knowing kind, kiddo!"

"Get in there."

They entered the office. On her way to her desk, Lin took two mango-flavored Bubbles O' Bliss® out of the mini-fridge and handed one to Rusty, whose eyebrows rose. "No caff injection?"

"I'm sure your report will provide all the excitement I can tolerate."

"Report, ha!" The manager sat down on the two-seat couch. "More like a tiny but crucial update."

"Go." She took two sips from the Bubbles O' Bliss® can and then leaned back in her Olkin® Spine of Steel® chair.

"The viscount's people have raised the offer and suggested a more palatable location. A neutral ground, if you wish. Magma. During tomorrow night's pixkin game. You see, the viscount is a co-owner of the Grunting—"

"The Grunting Hogs®. Yes, I know." Lin shifted in the chair. "Muskeg, I assume?"

Rusty nodded. "Lava® versus Hogs®."

Lin shifted again. "How much?"

"Money? A cool four mil."

"How long?"

"I got them down to one hour of interview time."

"And at no point will I be required to crawl into a dungeon dressed as a slutty troll or something?"

Rusty smiled. "Almost zero chance of dungeon traversal."

Lin shifted again in her chair.

"We'll send the burliest crew guys the station can find. If we're unhappy with the burliness level, I'll hire a few of my MMA guys out of my own pocket. You'll never be alone."

"What was he doing there anyway? What was he trying to accomplish with the stunt?" Jimmy had pulled up a chair next to the couch as he continued pressing Lucky Junior for info.

"From what I gathered—and mind you, he never gave me the whole picture—the momo was trying to extort the joint."

"Extort? For protection money?"

"Yeah. The folks there weren't budgin', so he figured he'd light a fire under their asses. Aw fuck, that came out messed up. But you know what I mean. Anyway, no one was supposed to get hurt. Just—y'know, scared into paying."

Jimmy lowered his head. "What a momo. What a mega-momo of a man. I keep hoping I'll wake up. How is this real?"

"Should we go to the cops?"

"Not yet. Let's see if **we** can find him first, maybe work out a deal."

"A deal with the law?" Lucky Junior shook his head. "There won't be any deal for old Tommy. Not after this."

"We might finagle something. At least to spare him a date with Old Sparky."

"Worth a shot. I hear death row ain't all it's cracked up to be."

"It ain't just—" Jimmy's Earwig® hummed. He had let a few other calls go to VM, but this one he'd have to take. It was his Told You So®[9] liaison. "Gimme a tick here, pressing biz." He stepped away from the chair and answered the call.

Without any preamble, his liaison launched into the post-show debrief. "You missed one Burrito Banderillero® activation. Plus, the Blowback™ shot was blocked by Buddy Four's melonhead for most of the night."

"That boy does own one enormous punkin. Gotta give him that."

"I would have liked to see more munching on your part. They've got a Kablamo Krunch® Spec Edish rolling out for the Tundra Thunder®."

"Just around the corner, I know."

---

9   Told You So®: Athenia's most popular content-creator site. It features both free and pay-per-view streams. WUWI subscription plans start at one zaler per week.

"So if you know, why aren't you munchin'? And don't say 'Coz I'm talking' again. You'll be talking to the lint in your wallet if those sponsors don't vibe the love."

"I thought Buddy Five munched for all of us. And then some."

"Ad money don't care about no damn Buddy Five. Was that clear enough for you? You're the only draw. And Tommy, when he's around. Everyone else is just expendable supporting cast."

"Like the bobbleheads in the den."

"Oh, that reminds me. I got an enticing propo from my guy over at Wobbling Noggins®. They've just come out with a BLOODBOIL® 4 tie-in line. I know you're a fan of those games, so it's not like you'd be soul selling. We take a few wobblers and sprinkle them around the place. One here, one there . . . Interested?"

"Tie me up, I guess. As long as it's not too blatant."

"No room for worries. It'll be just the right amount of blatancy. Those guys know two things: how to make wobblers and how to strategically place them. By the way, what's Tommy up to these days? Would he be willing to come back to the show?"

Jimmy felt his blood boil. He closed his eyes and sighed. "The chances of that happening are . . . slim."

"How do I get back here in time for the nine o'clock?" Lin asked.

"Company jet. You fly in, you fly out," Rusty said.

"On the wings of a dream."

"Piece o' cake."

Lin shifted in her chair. "How far from the airport—"

"Oh, Lin, I can't stand to watch you keep shifting in that thing." Rusty got off the couch. "Maybe the couch would agree with you more? I'll stand if need be."

"Listen to him, would ya? This is the Olkin® Spine of Steel® Series 7. The chair other chairs use to rest after a long day of chairing. I'm not shifting coz I'm uncomfy. I'm shifting coz I wanna get my money's worth, un-arch that crooked back."

"**Crooked? Your** back? Baby Lin, how can you even—"

She raised her palm. "Rusty! Zippy."

Rusty paused. "Zippy with trying to big you up? Or zippy completely, as in no words out of my piehole?"

"Just . . . enough with the 'Lin the Infallible' meltarama. What was I saying before you offered yourself as a human sacrifice?"

"You wanted to know how far away the airport is—from the stadium, I assume." Rusty one-cheeked himself on the couch armrest. "Forget all that. All the calculations have been done. All you need to do is be the best Lin Wesley you can be."

"Questions?"

"None from my side."

Lin grinned. "Have the interview questions been prepared?"

"In advance?! My innocence has just been shattered."

Lin slow-clapped. "I'll take that as a yes. Wardrobe? When will the money hit my account? What's the tax rate on this type of thing?"

"All valid questions to which I have the answers. Before I leap for joy, let me ask you this: provided you're happy with all the arrangements, will you do it?"

Lin finished her Bubbles O' Bliss® and bounced the can off the wall. "Magma or bust, baby!"

Rusty leaned over the desk and shook her hand. "You know it makes sense."

"What's there to lose, eh?"

"Only your integrity. Just kidding!"

"I'll have to reschedule some spots." She grabbed her cell phone and fired off a few messages, then used a burner phone to send one more SMS. "Was that a knowing smirk that flashed across my precious manager's mug?"

"Burner phone to send a text? You're single. It can basically mean only one thing."

The night before, she had spent a session with a good-time guy whose magic wand all the ladies in her inner circle kept raving about. She enjoyed the ride and had already made plans to go back for more.

"Rusty Blevins, the all-knowing seer."

"It's my job to know everything."

"I have a feeling I'll be hearing that line on a loop in the coming years."

"For as long as I have the pleasure of bullfighting for your best interests."

"Where were we?"

"Before you got a call? Tommy was getting all restless on death row."

"As I was saying," Jimmy re-took his seat next to Lucky Junior's couch, "it ain't just the cops that we need to worry about."

"Eh?"

"You're aware that the O'Reillys are one of the country's most powerful families, right?"

"Yeah."

"The rulers of Magma. The owners of our energy. It never occurred to you that they might want to seek justice outside of the 'proper channels?'" Jimmy air-quoted the last two words.

Lucky Junior sat up higher on the couch. "Like how?"

"Like hiring their own spec-ops-type mercs to hunt and destroy Tommy. Or even greasing the cops into blowing Tommy away the minute they find him."

"Cops can't just kill him cold. They got cameras now. They gotta behave."

"Here's some more food for thought. Say this drags on—the investigation, the search. Say they suspect Tommy, but he's nowhere to be found. How long—"

"They haven't even mentioned his name yet. At least not in public."

"How long before the O'Reilly goons turn to us for 'help?'"

"Us, like you and me?"

"They'll come knocking on my door as soon as they ID Tommy as a suspect, which shouldn't take long. I mean, he **was** trying to shake the place down. What if they find out you were with him that night?"

Lucky Junior shot up from the couch. "I ain't involved in this! I told him not to do it! It ain't fair!" He stormed out of the living room. "God damn that momo to goddamn fucking hell!"

Jimmy followed him into the kitchen. "No point in yelling. We are where we are. We gotta deal with the situation."

"I don't know where the fucker is!" Junior opened and closed drawers and cabinets, the cutlery singing its blaring rattle with each shuttering bang.

"Uh-huh. And how many days on the torture rack will they make us spend before they're satisfied we really know nothing?"

"Fuck! **Daaaaad!**"

Lucky Senior walked down from the upper floor. "Mad at knives and forks now, are we?"

"Jimmy thinks the O'Reillys might send their goons after us. Help!"

"What is this, amateur dinner theater?" Lucky Senior jerked his thumb at the living room. "Back in there, the both o' youse!"

Jimmy and Junior took a seat at either end of the couch. Senior leaned against the chair. "You like my 'threads,' as the kids say?"

Jimmy nodded. "Very nice."

"Spot on," his son agreed.

"I hemmed and hawed for ten minutes in front of the closet upstairs before settling on this combo. There's a saucy new widow in town, been hitting the bar lately. I caught her giving me the old smolder eye on multiple occasions, too often to consider it a fluke. Today is the day I go in for the kill."

"As the kids say."

"How can you be sure she'll be in today?"

"Feel it in my bones, as **Jimmy** says. See? I'm still hip. Plus, it's her regular afternoon outing slot."

"Ehm . . . Pops? The O'Reillys. Our necks in the noose. Any ideas?"

"Plenty." Lucky Senior stepped out into the hall to grab his jacket. "But none of them good." He put on the jacket and reappeared in front of the couch where the two youngsters were hand-wringing and head-sinking.

"Would you look at these two." He shook his head. "Sons of Levski. Balls of steel. We bleed blue, and so will you. Not an inch or dig your ditch.[10] More like, hold me close as I quiver like a rose."

"Hey, that doesn't rhyme."

Senior grinned at Jimmy. "Well, **you** would know, Mister 'I watch other men do stuff and talk over it.'"

The WUWI star shrugged. "That's where the money is these days."

Senior dismissed him with a hand wave and addressed Junior: "How long before the cops ID Tommy as the perp?"

"Ballpark figure? Not long."

There was a minute of silence, broken by Senior: "You forgot how to talk? I oughta get the belt, go old-school on your ass."

"I'm a grown man!"

---

10   Historic Levski Point social upheaval slogans.

"Mooching off my teet. Warping my beautiful couch with your hideous bottom. So, you better quit the pidgin for a smidgen. Why 'not long?'"

"He was trying to shake down the owners of the donut shop. They laughed in his face, so he went jungle warfare on them."

"I know the owners. They paid for their freedom decades ago. Tommy can consider himself lucky they didn't turn the tables and sic some street guy on him. That fuckin' momo." Lucky Senior turned to leave.

"Pops, some of those lowlifes who hang around your joint? Maybe you can ask them if they heard something, help us track him down."

"Sure. Hey, wait a minute. Who you calling 'lowlifes?' Those people paid for the roof over your knuckly head. You insult them again, I'll take away your fridge privilege."

"Thanks for the help, Mister Malanga." Jimmy stood up. "For everything. This ain't your fight, I know. We'll find Tommy soon. I'm sorry that idiot brought this drama into your house."

"Family, eh?" Senior grinned at him.

"Where would we be without them?"

7 Conviction

The halogen lights in the interview room flickered and hummed as Hieronymus Kelski sat at a wobbly table and pondered his next move.

Just as he was about to rerun the scenario gamut from the top, the door opened, and the assistant public defender (APD) entered the small room.

"Can't y'all do nuthin about them flickery wickedries? Or is that one of your sly mindbender techniques, trying to crack old Kelski?"

The APD placed his briefcase on the table and his wraparound bag on the floor next to his chair. "No need for theatrics, Mr. Kelski. We both know you're an educated man who switches the 'backwoods rube' persona on and off as it suits him." He sat opposite the suspect and rolled up his sleeves.

"Well, spank me blue and call me Stu! Looks like they sent one of them brain-equipped drones."

"Again, Mr. Kelski, no need for the gold prospector act. We'll give the lights another five mins. They should cut out the flickering by then. If not, I'll buzz the guards."

"What **is** this place? Some kinda futuristic palace?"

"As you're well aware, this is the Ploughburg East AUIM facility. You will be held here until your post-arrest status is finalized. Hopefully today, after our consultation here." The APD took a notepad and two folders out of his briefcase.

"What's in the bag?" Kelski foot-nudged the APD's wraparound bag.

"Please don't kick the bag." The APD made a note in his notepad, then closed the briefcase and put it on the floor next to the bag. "Now, then. You—"

"The contents of the bag shall remain a mystery to old Kelski? For his mind to be titillated and drained? So it grows weak and is unable to put up a fight against the forces of the law? Is that the game we're playing, dearest APD?"

"No games being played here, Mr. Kelski. Just a good old-fashioned post-arrest suspect assessment protocol."

"PASAP?"

"Indeed! Are you familiar with it?"

"Not from personal experience. Until now. But you already knew that."

"Quite." The APD jotted down a few more words in his notepad. "You were already advised of this, but it's worth repeating that everything in this room is being recorded, video and audio."

"Where is it? The camera."

"There are several of them, one in each corner." The APD pointed with his pencil to a corner above Kelski's head. "Ultra-high quality."

"Was there ever any doubt? Only the best for the Ministry."

"Not for the Ministry. For the people of Athenia. Please also bear in mind that none of the footage captured here can be used against you, as we have a confidentiality bond. The footage is deleted two hours after the interview, unless one or both parties feel there were problems with the interview."

Old Man Kelski yawned. "Reckon I can get a mini-cig in here?"

"You can. But you can't smoke it."

"Alright, I'll play along. I crave me a stumpy. If I don't get one, I'll clam up."

The APD hand-darted into his wraparound bag and produced a high-end mini-cig. "One crisp cigar for Mr. Kelski."

"Damn near fell outta my cold hard chair just now!" The old man snatched the mini-cig and pulled a hooter-vacuum over it, relishing the aroma. "Holiest of molies, you **did** come prepared. In tune with all of Kelski's foibles and spoilerds."

"As long as we get to the truth."

"You won't get any truth-jammers from me." Kelski admired the cigar's texture. "Only thing is, you might not believe what I tell you."

"I've been in this crazy business we call law for over a decade. There's nothing I haven't seen or heard."

"Like a doctor, jaded from all the assholes."

The APD made another note in his notepad. "Okay. You've been arrested—"

"What are you writing in there?" Kelski sniffed the mini-cig.

"It's just for my reference. I wanted to jot down a few points while the file is still fresh in the old noggin."

"Don't go forgetting stuff. My life is hanging in the balance."

"Not your life but certainly your freedom. You've been arrested under suspicion of prisoner harboring. That's a spicy meatball of a crime."

"As it should be. Throw away the key."

"Upon arrest, you indicated to the officers that, and I quote, 'I ain't seen Klenny in a dozen man years at a minimum.' Do you maintain your innocence?"

"I maintain." Kelski closed his eyes and twirled the cigar under his nose.

"Guide me thru your day. Saturday, the day of the arrest. When did you wake up?"

Kelski stayed shtum as he continued to sniff the mini-cig.

"Mr. Kelski? Sir?"

"Don't think me rude. I'm merely pondering how I might save the both of us a whole bunch of time."

"Best way to save time? Telling the truth."

Kelski opened his eyes. "I was framed by the AUIM."

"Guess it's time for **me** to play along. How and why did the AUIM frame you?"

"Money, I assume. That's the why of it. Not sure yet about the how. How they snuck in Klenny and the others without me twiggin'."

"The AUIM snuck Klenny's group into your basement?"

Kelski nodded. "Must've happened while I was out that day. Collecting firewood."

"You do that yourself? Why not order from a supplier?"

"It ain't the money, if that's what you're driving at. Roaming around them woods puts me in the right thinking mode. Makes them twiggies useful for a change."

"According to the file, you're known to have a special bond with the forest around your home. But now you're saying it feels like a burden?"

Kelski stopped twirling the mini-cig. "A 'special bond?' Seems that brain they equipped you with might be in desperate need of some fresh batteries."

"Help me understand, if you don't mind."

Kelski resumed smelling the cigar. "Do you know how the Kelski clan wound up at the Local Road 34 homestead?"

"Yes."

"Liar."

"It's pronounced 'lawyer.'"

"Oh, look, he's a comedian too. Meanwhile, I'm fighting for my life. Sorry, 'freedom.'"

"I apologize. But I **do** know your family's history. Still fresh." The APD tapped the folder.

"Well, I'd like to use this opportunity to expand on the knowledge you claim to possess. To paint a more vivid picture, if you like. And not coz I enjoy the sound of my own voice—a very fine voice though it might be. I just wanna make sure you understand the context of old Kelski's attitude."

"Yes, sir. Do go on."

"During the penultimate year of the Pacification Wars, Harrington's armies were—"

"Pardon the interruption, Mr. Kelski, but as I said, I'm familiar with the file. Not to mention that every Athenian child, including me, learns about the Pike Valley Massacre in third grade."

"**Paint a picture!**" Kelski multi-stabbed the air with the stumpy. "That's what I'll do, whether a certain assistant public defender finds it to his liking or not! Coz right now, painting fucking pictures is all I have. You've gone and pulled the old clang and bang on my wrinkly ass in a breathtaking stitch-up, so now you'll sit there and indulge this here old fart as he paints some heart-stringy pictures!"

The APD scribbled in his notepad.

"It was crucial for Harrington's troops to link up with Teixeira's Second Infantry at Pike Valley. As in, link up or face annihilation. The rebels were flooding in, drunk on moonshine and bloodlust, the defeat at Klugno still fresh in their minds. Like my folder is fresh in yours."

"Mr. Kelski—"

"**Ten men!**" Kelski slammed his palm on the table. "Ten men—eight men and two women, to be exact—held off a division for three days. Let me say it again, in case whoever is monitoring all these camera feeds missed it." He windmilled his arm at the corners of the room. "Ten people, none of them pro soldiers, bogged down an eight-thousand-strong division using nothing but guile and terrain mastery."

"They had weapons too."

"Would you listen to—**of course they had weapons!** Orangutan im Größenwahn, talk about missing the bloody point. They were sniping, booby trapping, harassing. Ten versus eight thousand. Many a rebel became convinced they were dealing with ghosts, throwing their minds for a loop. Even if they survived physically, they were gone mentally."

"Nothing more superstitious than a soldier in a trench."

"When the bastards finally broke thru, they got the news that Harrington had linked up with Teixeira and gained the upper hand in the region. As they retreated, they took revenge on the local populace, no matter the allegiance. Everyone was branded fair game, including women and kids. They'd make moms hold their babies and jump off cliffs. They'd make—"

"Mr. Kelski, we don't—"

"You know how many people survived? Out of two thousand?"

"They don't call them the Pike Valley Eight for nothing. Again, I went to school, remember?"

"Eight." Kelski nodded. "Including a couple of Kelskis. After the war, the authorities awarded the government-owned land around Cowherd's Pike to those eight people. That's how my family wound up at the homestead we all know and love."

"Speaking of which, what makes—"

"The very homestead your goons ripped me out from over the weekend." Kelski resumed sniffing the mini-cig.

"They're not **my** goons—or **anyone's**, for that matter."

"Sure. They're the brave ministry officers, watching over us and keeping us safe."

"Getting back to the statement you made earlier, what makes you think you were framed?"

"They want to build a pipeline."

"They?"

"Who else? The Magma mafia."

"I see. They asked for permission to use your land but you refused?"

"Damn straight. I chinned up to those masters of the universe with their steely gazes and silly blazers. Ain't no one knows what kinda poison them pipes gonna be carrying, neither Mars nor devil." Kelski smirked. "As my rube persona would put it."

"They paid you a visit at your property?"

"Several."

"Properties?"

"Visits. One home is all I got and all I need. But they can't let a man enjoy his castle in peace."

"You're worried that the substance planned to be shipped thru the pipeline might endanger your health?"

"And overall well-being, yes. It'd be preying on my mind, see? Constantly eating away at the ol' gray matter." Kelski made a circular motion with the cigar, pointing at his temple.

"What type of fuel is it?"

Kelski froze. "Something just dawned on me. Up and clobbered this tired old noggin sitting on my neck. When the cops showed up at my door, I threw some silly line at the lady cop."

"Officer Paulson."

"And just as she exploded with laughter, we heard a noise from the basement. I took that to be peculiar. I mean, a ministry chick doubling over at my dumb jokes? No wings on **that** pig."

"You think that was the signal for Klenny to reveal the group's location?"

Kelski paused and marinated. "Yes. I'm calling it. That was the signal."

"What would be in it for the escapees? What would they gain, aside from more years tacked onto their sentences?"

"RED ORE® has unlimited funds. They can pay each of them millions for those extra years behind bars."

"That's quite a yarn."

"Oh, the rube is spinning yarns, is he? Here's another nail in your coffin of justice, Mister Assistant." Kelski popped the mini-cig behind his ear and leaned in close. "Does it say anything in the folder about eminent domain and the fact that my property is immune to it? Does it mention circumstances in which my property **could** be legally taken away from me? Like, um, oh, lemme think, harboring fugitives? Bingo!"

"Which brings us to the heart of the matter—the charge you've been saddled with. It's quite a whopper, as we've already agreed."

Kelski leaned back and folded his arms across his chest.

"There's a handful of scenarios that can result in your land being taken away from you, and harboring fugitives is one of them. It's considered treason, a betrayal of the same country that gave you the land in the first place."

"The land drenched in the blood of my ancestors."

"Quite. Which is why—"

"Which is why I would never in a zillion years do anything to blight their sacrifice. Hiding Klenny the clown and his buddies? Why would I pull such a bone-header?"

"The law is not concerned with the logic, or lack thereof, of your actions. The only thing relevant to your case is whether the prosecution can prove your guilt. And let me tell you, based on everything I've heard and seen so far, they've got you bang to rights."

"Did they say why the pretzel van was on the premises?"

"'They,' being Glendale Oax® officials, issued a statement saying the van was delivering catering supplies for a retiring warder's farewell party."

"You're being serious?"

The APD shuffled thru the folder, then pulled out a paper and offered it to Kelski. "Feast your eyes on a crisp copy."

"I ain't wasting the last of my eyesight on their flights of fancy. Here's another head scratcher: why did it take them a full day to come out with this farewell party explanation?"

"It was a surprise party. The guvner was unaware."

"OK, but a whole day? How does he communicate with his staff? Carrier pigeon?"

"I assume they were embarrassed and were hoping for a quick end to the drama. Now that the piggies are back in the pen, the flak from the public will be much smaller."

"Had a buddy who did a stint in Glendale a few years back. There's a thing called the Guvner's Dozen. Ever heard of it?"

"No evidence was ever found."

"So you **did** hear." Kelski put the mini-cig on the table and stretched. "Basically, it's a weekly cut of the booming prison economy which must be kicked up to Corrigan. Originally, it was around thirteen K. I would imagine it's a lot higher now."

"If they had a hall of fame for guvners, Corrigan would be a first-ballot inductee. No good being a squeaky-clean guvner if the inmates burn down your prison."

"Once again, way to miss the point."

"Which is?"

"The man is as crooked as a snake's spleen. Must've been in on the stitch-up."

"The net widens."

"Wouldn't be shocked to learn that he owns a piece of the pretzel firm."

"Get It Twisted™? Ever tried them?"

"No."

"I did this morning. Sampled a cinnamon one. Not bad. A new . . . twist."

"Well la-di-da. Meanwhile, I'm still rotting in here."

"The one-day delay suggests they were **not** in on it. Otherwise, they'd have had an excuse ready and waiting."

"The old 'if they're scrambling, they ain't conspiring' defense."

"I'll have to remember that one." The APD made a note.

They sat in silence for a bit.

"What else is in the bag?"

"You want another cigar?"

Kelski waved it off, then leaned back and closed his eyes. "LRO."

"Laughing . . . my . . . rump off?"

Kelski smirked. "Liquefied Red Ore. You asked about the name of the fuel. That's the name. The next big thing. The new magic potion. The silver bullet to cure everything that ails us."

"Never heard of it."

"You will. They're keeping it hush-hush until they've got all the pieces in place. Once they do, get ready for a media storm that will blow away any remaining pockets of resistance."

"Such as yourself?"

"They don't need the media to stooge **me** up. I'm already locked up, ain't I?"

"Mr. Kelski, you've had a long history of vetoing proposals concerning the commercial development of the LR 34 area, to the point of alienating all of your neighbors. They see your attitude as an obstacle to a better life. Many have moved out; there's hardly a young person left. Isn't your blocking of the pipeline just another way to stick it to your neighbors?"

Kelski opened his eyes. "Do I need to start painting pictures again?"

The APD raised his palm. "No more pictures, thank you. You cite honoring your ancestors as the main reason for not wanting commercial activity around LR 34, but—"

"No **new** commercial developments. You give those hyenas an inch and within a fortnight you'll have an amusement park in your backyard. Screaming kids and shitstained lids."

"But you've approved proposals when it has suited you. Wider roads, more convenient fuel stations, lumber yard expansion, Interregional Rail Network® link, stockfeed distribution center, **second** lumber yard expansion, and . . . This can't be right, a helipad?"

"With a big yellow H."

"Who builds a helipad without owning a helicopter?"

"A poor man with big dreams."

"Those dreams, Mr. Kelski . . ." The APD reached into his bag and pulled out a shiny leather folder. "Are about to burst."

"Turtle in a girdle, could this be the end of the mystery bag drama?"

"Due to your advanced age and clean record, the government will recommend a twenty-year sentence of house arrest." The APD placed the folder in front of Kelski. "In exchange for a guilty plea. That's a mighty generous offer."

"'Advanced age.' You say it like it's a disease."

"All you need to do is sign and initial. The spots are labeled."

"What happens to my property rights?"

"They revert to the Central Government."

"Sonsabitches."

"The evidence against you is overwhelming. If you opt for a trial, you'll be found guilty, lose your property rights just the same, and die in prison. With this deal, you get to go back home within a week, right after you stand before the judge."

"What if the judge disagrees with the recommendation?"

"They won't."

Kelski palm-buried his face. "I didn't do this. I was framed. Can't you see that?"

"The offer is valid until midnight. I can come back later if you need time to think it over."

"What guarantees me they won't throw me out of my home? It'll belong to them, after all."

"Page four. Should such a situation arise, there's a provision saying the CG will need to provide accommodation on par with your current residence."

"How often am I allowed to leave the house?"

"That's up to the judge. But the legal minimum is one hour of open air per day."

"What about my pension?"

"Also up to the judge. I've seen it taken away, left as is, and everything in between."

"The pipeline?"

"Should they choose to build one, they will need permission from the CG. You won't have a say in the matter."

Kelski sat in silence, staring into the distance.

"They can have their fucking pipeline." He whipped open the folder and looked up at a camera. "Hope you choke on it."

8 Moon

The neon sign of Tuff Guy Tavern lit up the Herzland night, a shining beacon for tourists casually dressed and truckers catching a quick rest.

In the sprawling parking lot behind the restaurant, a We Haul Gas® truck awoke with a diesel rumble. The driver stretched, yawned, mirror checked, buckled up, slapped his cheeks, glanced at the bundles of joy in the shotgun seat, and pulled out of his stall.

He was in the home stretch of a weeklong slog, loading cargo at the local megastation before dispensing it to fueling points around Farmer Dale's® region. He was tired but less than usual, owing to a storm cleanup that had closed the roads the previous night. He got an unheard-of eight hours of sleep!

He touch-tested the coffee cup in the cupholder—five or so minutes until it was cool enough to drink. He had learned his road coffee lessons the hard way. *If I had a nickel for every burnt tongue and stained shirt . . .*

He sat back and cruised thru a crisp night, the round, reddish moon glimmering above the forest lining the road. Another glance at the shotgun seat. *Can't wait to see their faces.* He tugged on the cord above him, and the air horn gave a happy hoot to reflect his good mood.

He was approaching the exit that would take him into what he dubbed "Ghostly Plains." In all the deliveries he had made to that fuel depot, he had never seen any other vehicles around. The farmhands assigned to the area worked during the day and left in the evening while his schedule had him deliver there only at night. He did the math. If he bagged the stop quickly, he might beat the morning rush-hour traffic, drop the last few loads by noon, and be home a full day early. *A dream worth fighting for if there ever was one.* He sent a shot of just-right-temperature java down his throat, warrior wiggled in his seat, then focused on the road and added ten miles to the speedometer.

"That, in a nutshell, is how we see the inverse derivation devaluation benefiting all the stakeholders," Cynthia Lennox said, concluding her final pitch for the day.

"It wouldn't work on the regional level," the CGR said. "National, yes. Yorba Woods, yes. And other Terra Liberas too, for that matter. But not for the provinces. They would lose a lot and gain a little."

"Even if a more stringent leverage interpretation were applied?"

"You'd need approval from each affected province. Or a victorious legislative battle. None of which is likely."

"I suspected as much. Still, better to have it off the table than in the dreamworld."

The CGR leaned back in silence.

"What is it?"

"I've seen many a peddler walk thru that door over the years. You're still a rookie at this level of haggling, but you're a natch. I'm not just blowing smoke. You ask anybody about the lady from Room 499, and they'll tell ya—nothing but straight shootin' and Filibuster[11] rootin'."

"What about flag salutin'?"

---

11   Harrington Filibusters®: The capital city's APL® franchise.

"When the mood strikes. Usually around the holiday bonus season."

"I feel there's a pregnant 'but' menacing above us."

The CGR laughed. "You're a natch, but your heart wasn't in this pitch."

"The last one? I knew it was hinky due to the entrenched interests likely bellyaching. Still . . . it's a good plan."

"On a desert island. Not in the real world. Here, bellyaching is king."

"If only we **were** on a desert island. No need for wrangling over regulation."

The CGR mock-clutched her heart. "Why you gotta hurt me so bad?! After all I've done for you."

Cynthia clapped with delight.

"'No regulation,' she says. Tsk, tsk. That lone palm tree keeping you company on your desert island? Say a coconut falls from the tree and clunks you on the noggin. Without regulation, you wouldn't even know who to sue. Then you'd come crawling right back to the lady from Room 499, crying over out-of-control coconuts in desperate need of regulation."

Cynthia doubled over with laughter. "How'd I get back to Harrington so fast?"

"In a fit of murderous revenge-fueled rage, you cut down the poor old palm tree—the only true friend you ever had on the island—and fashioned a raft. It was creaky but reliable."

"And on that raft, I surfed back to the regulated world."

"Score one for the good guys!"

"Poisonous Pelican to De-striped Tiger, come in, over."

"Knock it off with the knockoff wisecrackery, son-in-law number five. It ain't you."

"Care to share—"

"You hear me say 'over?'"

Silence.

"Over."

"Tip of the old hat, father-in-law numero one. Care to share the reasoning behind this late birdie wing you're undertaking?"

"A man can't survey his blood-fed lands no more? When'd they ban **that** one?"

"No ban on surveying. But why past sunset?"

"The night is crisp. And look at that moon!"

"That is one mighty fine glowin' orb, ain't no denyin'. Still . . ."

"Out with the tar, Randy old boy. Freshen up those lungs!"

"I'm clamped under this non-pleasant heaviness, like something ain't right tonight."

"Where? At the farm?"

"In your heart."

Farmer Dale glided across the skies in his Bug Bomber® crop duster, clearing his head as he sprayed chemicals on select patches of land. "Just sprayin' and slayin'. Ain't no room for heaviness in **this** here ticker."

"Glad to hear. Even though doubts are still a-creepin'."

"Coz that's what they do, Randy, me son. They creep and they crawl till they've built a big ol' doubt-filled sprawl. Boom! Take that, wannabe vermin!"

Randy was stunned into silence.

"Not even a chuckle?"

"Why you gotta go all atomic on poor Randy H. like that?"

"What in—oh, I wasn't war-cryin' at you, solid son-in-law. Just dropped a load over Sector 13, put the fear of Mars into any critter fixing to foment."

"How many rounds you plannin' to fly?"

"Thinkin' a couple more. Let the moon be my shepherd."

The We Haul Gas® driver double-checked the gauge monitoring system, slammed the nozzle receptors shut, code-locked the Ghostly Plains fuel tank, and hopped back into his warm cab.

Too warm, he decided. If he got too comfy, he might drift into dreamland, followed by a slide into deadland. He dialed back the heater and downed the rest of his coffee. As soon as he did, he reached for his Hixville Herd®-branded stainless steel insulated bottle and replenished his cup with a fresh round of brew.

He pulled a beauty of a U-turn. The mighty truck cleared the tree branches on the right and the farm equipment on the left in under ten ticks. *So long, Ghostly Plains!*

As he rumbled down the narrow road leading to the highway, he ran the remaining route thru his head one more time. Definitely doable to make it home earlier, he concluded and sped up a notch. His confidence was boosted by the helping hand provided by the zesty moon. *Here's lookin' at ya, Pumpkin!*

He snuck another peek at the treasure in the shotgun seat and smiled from coast to coast. Next thing he knew, the truck was careening down a long ravine while fresh coffee was frying his face.

"I take it you've gone off the casino kick?" the CGR asked Cynthia.

"Affirmative. Too many moving parts and divergent interests. It'd probably take years. The viscount wasn't keen on it to begin with. Maybe we'll revisit it at some point."

"So, back to square one? After all that time and effort?"

Cynthia sat up in her chair. "Crossing things off the list. That's valuable too. Keeps us bearing down on the grand prize."

"Like greyhounds chasing that big juicy rabbit."

"Yeah, a rabbit worth a trillion."

"Spoken to Gary yet?"

"Gary? Oh, the Board guy. It seems we might be in business with those carbon credits. Nice little earner on the side. But as you said, it doesn't solve our main issue."

"At least you got something. Don't forget, there are new schemes and dreams bubbling up all the time. Like yeast. Stuff seemingly out of the leftest of fields can suddenly click right into your chamber."

"Cocked the old six-shooter ages ago. Just scanning for that magic bullet."

"It's out there somewhere."

"Wish it'd give a hoot already." Cynthia shuffled her papers and then returned them to her briefcase. "And/or a holler."

"Alas, it's a shy bugger. Off in a secluded corner, smiling its faint grin."

"You got time for a few Qs on education?"

"School is in sesh."

"How's that new feed holdin' up? Hogs dig it?"

"That's a negative, Flyin' Dale. Was gonna suggest one more week of tryouts before we boomerang it back where it came from."

"Where **did** it come from?" Dale asked as he swooped over a cornfield and unleashed the Bug Bomber® cargo.

"Name is eluding. Sumkinda government-backed initiative. Produced in Aurelia."

"Soon as I hear 'government' has a neighbor called 'initiative,' I know it's time to call the Reaper."

"Coz the thing is dead in the water?"

"Dead and buried, Randy old chum, dead and—turtle in a girdle, did the kids take care of the woodchippery like they were s'posed to?"

"Just keep sprinkling that magic dust in peace, De-striped Tiger. They did as ordered."

"Confirmed visual?"

"Young Karl sent pics. Woodchippery collected and secured."

"Coz if they didn't, you know what's brewing on that gray horizon, dontcha? Mother Maci will up and press that Turbo Nag button. Hate to see kids cry."

"If she presses that big button, we'll all be weeping, young and old."

"Hey, you notice we stopped saying 'over?'"

"'Over' is overrated."

The We Haul Gas® driver drifted back into consciousness, unsure how long he'd been out.

He saw airbags all around him. *Is that what did it? Did the airbags knock me out?*

The engine had been humming in Accident Autopilot mode. He killed it and then eye-spied for the overhead clock but saw only mangled wires where the clock once was. *Can I turn my neck?* Turned out he could. A brief scan of the cabin revealed it was one heck of a wreck.

Up next, his mug began to brim with heat.

The coxucking coffee. It had splashed on him when the truck flew off the road—the last thing he remembered before waking up. He rubbed his cheek.

That better not be swelling! Hang on, maybe that's what woke me up. The pain from the burn. Maybe java is my ally after all.

He propped himself up in the seat, and that's when the **real** injury hammered him, flashing lights and all. He looked down and saw the source of his misery. His left leg had gone kaput in two places—below the knee and at the ankle.

Son of a whore from a syphilitic shore!

The pain was so bad, he considered weeping. Then he forced his brain to slow down for a minute.

Flush out the panic flow, noble trucking hero. The pain ain't so bad; you're just crazy mad. It's the frustration, not the sensation. How'd I flip the fucking truck?! Over a decade hauling shit up and down and to and fro and never an at-cause accident, and now all I'm—flush it out, goddammit!

He managed to slow his breathing and halt the onslaught of dark thoughts, but then another one ricocheted in his head: what if he lost consciousness again and never woke up?

He howled in agony as he reached for the dangling Earwig® attached to the console. Once the gizmo was in his hand, he savored the small triumph for a moment before clicking the HQ button.

Nothing.

He hit it again.

No lights flashed.

Again. This time he pressed every single button.

No lights or sounds.

How the fuck is that possible? These things usually break only when the truck explodes.

Hoping to give the electronics a jolt, he restarted the engine and despair-whacked the comm a few more times.

Dead as a doornail.

And soon I'll be too.

". . . teacher pensions. Those strikes four years ago? That's what was at the heart of it. It had nothing to do with protecting poor pupils from the scourge of Expanded History."

"I knew it!" Cynthia slapped the desk. "How is the expansion going, by the way? I mean, my kids keep me up to speed, but how are things looking from the CG's angle?"

The CGR shrugged. "We were hoping for more progress at this stage. Some minds are clamped shut."

"Surely the CG has no shortage of crowbars."

"Plenty of crowbars, not enough brains. But you didn't hear that from me."

"If only they could clone an army of Room 499 ladies. Talk about expansion!"

"Sweet. But only after I'm gone and buried please. A thousand extra relatives overnight? Showing up unannounced at my house with their taped-up coolers and tales of woe? Might as well jump out the window right now."

Cynthia laughed. "I see it more as a general commanding an army. 'You, shine my boots! You, go stand over there! You number three, where's my frozen yogurt?'"

The CGR thumbed-up. "Uncanny."

Cynthia reached for her cell phone. "What say I clone us up a couple or four Breaker Breaker! Breakfasts from Donut Depot®? As a reward for a job not done."

The CGR blinked. "Did you say 'four?' Are you saying you're looking to devour two ginormo-breakfasts by yourself? Or even three?"

"All crunch and no munch makes Cynthia a hoggish gal."

"I'll say. Better hit that portion-control button, or you'll be oinking with the best of them."

"If the button doesn't work, there's always the e-brake. In the shape of my index finger."

"Ew!"

"Two Breaker Breakers it is, then. We'll keep it civil. Plus a Cauldron o' Coffee®."

"How could we even **think** of eschewing the Cauldron?"

"Do you consider these negotiations failed?"

"I do."

"No sugar coating from **this** lady, eh?"

"Room 499. Where lies come to die."

"I still say we're close. Much closer than we give ourselves credit. We just need that one spark."

"When it ignites, holla. I'll be here, waiting for all this chow you're feeding me to be expelled from my system in a violent diarrhea."

"One of these days," Cynthia said as she clicked the order into her phone. "One of these days."

Turns out death ain't so bad. Not sure what all the drama is about. You just gotta put one foot in and one foot out.

The We Haul Gas® driver could already see glimmers of distant galaxies calling out to him, enticing celestial travelers with promises of far-flung reaches of the ever-expanding universe offering rejoinders to the deepest of quandaries and powers of wisdom bestowment the likes of which only but the tiniest of fractions of humanity had ever even dared to dream attainable.

What about this fucking leg, though? I can hear my angel wings behind me, flapping with excitement, but how can I spread them when my GD leg is shattered and stuck? Nothing left to do but reach out to HQ for advice.

He grabbed a chunk of air and slumped back in disappointment.

Oops, mustn't upset my angel wings. Better sit up straight. Oh no, I can't coz of the leg! Alright, high time to rev up the wings and find safe harbor far away from this scrap heap. On three! One . . . two . . . Precious angel wings, why aren't you revving? And not only that, you're also emitting a troubling sickly metallic sound, as if there's a—

The sound of breaking glass yanked the trucker back into a conscious state. Back to the sad reality of his wobbled wheels and pulsating pain. He rolled his eyes to the left and saw a dark figure outside the window, observing him. He tried to draw attention to his injury but mustered only gibberish. The figure loomed closer to the window and raised its right hand.

Is that an ax?!

As the object hurtled toward his face, the driver turned away and braced for impact, but none came. Instead, shattered glass flew into the cabin, followed by a pair of hands grabbing him by the collar and pulling him up in the seat.

"Commander Simons, Interior Ministry! We're getting you out of here!"

"My leg . . . it's busted . . ."

"We'll get it fixed! Show me your eyes!" Simons grabbed the driver's head and peered into his peepers. "Can you hear me? Do you understand what I'm saying?"

"Yes. Now. But I won't stay awake for long."

Simons reached thru the hole in the window, pressed the unlock button, then opened the door. "You ready? On three."

The driver closed his eyes and gritted his teeth, anticipating blackout-level pain.

"One."

"Two."

"**Heave!**"

The two men stumbled away from the truck. Unable to use his bum leg, the trucker lost his balance and started a nosedive toward the sloshy ground. Just before the point of no return, he felt a shoulder underneath his armpit, stopping his descent.

"Gotcha!" a female voice said.

"Lieutenant Paulson to the rescue!" Simons said. "As usual."

"All in a day's work."

"Honest work. Earning our bread."

"Alive not dead."

When the trio reached the AUIM off-roader, the cops helped the victim into the backseat, and Paulson took the wheel.

"Nearest shpitz, Lieutenant, double time." Simons was about to take a seat next to the trucker when the man spoke: "Please . . . for my babies . . . in the truck . . ."

"There are babies in the truck, sir?"

"For my kids . . . please . . . shotgun seat."

The cops exchanged looks. Simons shrugged, then sprinted back to the truck. He zapped a flashlight, saw the plastic bags, retrieved them along with his ax, then raced back to the off-roader.

Once back inside, he showed the bags to the trucker: "Is **this** your card?"

The man smiled and nodded. "Thank you, thank you, thank you."

Paulson hit the gas and the flashing lights.

"I gotta see this." Simons unfurled one of the bundles and couldn't help but grin. "Okulthor's Lunar Firebase™. Went on a toy run, did we?"

"For my kids. These are hard to find. Toys Aren't Toys® exclusive."

"Now, how come Okulthor® is living on the moon?" Paulson asked.

"You don't know?" Simons was taken aback. "His punk ass was chased out of Fort Fist® by none other than AbsorBlow® during the latest Tide Rise®."

The trucker winced in pain. "The ministry . . . follows Doomers of Gloom®?"

"The ministry follows everything."

9 Game Face

"Tim**berrrr!**"

Augustus "Ox" O'Reilly greeted Tim Phillips from the tufted leather armchair next to the wet bar off the side of his desk.

"Sir." Tim smiled and nodded, crossing the floor of RED ORE®'s second-grandest office. "Quite a lavish greeting, if I may say so. In these dark days."

"If you planned on shedding a tear for old Luke, don't. He was a burden to everyone. It was just a matter of time before he killed another tute or ran over another child."

"Those drunken stupors of his."

"They'd have locked him up ages ago if it weren't for the O'Reilly muscle." Ox puff-puff-puffed on a stubby and pointed to the twin armchair across from him. "Do make yourself comfy, old boy. Sensing a medium-length meeting here. We need to address the Luke demise aftermath no matter what we may have thought of him privately. Potential playoff implications, as the kids say."

Tim slumped into the plush leather and frowned. "Do I smell chocolate?"

Ox seemed pleased. "Indeed you do, dearest counterintelligence master!" He raised the dark stubby. "Choco-infused cigars. What **will** they think of next?"

"Any good?"

"The only reason I ain't retching right now is your presence."

"Whoa! And yet you keep puffing?"

Ox shrugged. "My youngest daughter's husband's latest venture. Gotta fly the flag."

"Why not flush 'em?"

"Last time I did that, it clogged the bloody toilet. When word got back to my wife, I had to sit thru a month of operas to prove my repentance."

"The second-most-powerful man in Magma. Maybe the country. And you can't even enjoy a decent cigar."

"Gotta puff on something." Ox sent a blast of smoke into the air, then coughed for a dozen ticks.

"Why not tell her you quit the glimmees?"

"Then she'd **know** I'm lying."

"My secretary's the same way. She's been with me for ages. Can't put anything past her."

"Oh yeah, Margie the Magnificent. She followed you up here all the way from AC."

"A job's a job. We were both out of meaningful work."

Tim got his BA at Remington, then got scooped up in the annual net trawl by ADA[12] where he was trained in skullduggery. Five years into a stellar spook career, his college BFF Steve Barton came calling with visions of venture capital grandiosity. He was looking to boost his well-funded start-up with Tim's intel-gathering and intel-shielding prowess. The dough was too much to say no. After the company folded, he helped run data protection (and/or destruction) for AC's rich and infamous. That was how he met Neil Zorich, who floated his name to Luke O'Reilly once the RED ORE® job became open. Augustus O'Reilly was keen on hiring an out-of-the-Magma-bubble intel expert. He considered all the local candidates too chummy with the established power structures. A new mind with a new set of eyes for a new tomorrow. Or something to that effect.

---

12 Athenian Defense Agency: The country's top national security agency.

"Rat?"

"Caught."

Ox extended his palm. Tim took out an envelope from his RED ORE® jacket pocket and placed it in the VP's hand.

Ox popped the cigar in a corner of his mouth, opened the envelope, and unfolded a sheet of paper. He read the text, rewound the envelope process, and tucked the proverbial clattering grenade in his blazer pocket. "Where is he?"

"Now? At home. Prepping for work."

"You got people watching him?"

Tim nodded. "Twenty-four/seven."

Ox paused. "Our top engineer is working what, the late shift?"

"Occasionally. Says it helps him think. As he's bending laws of nature to his will."

"Away from all those pesky humans."

"With their pointless baby slash vacation stories."

"All gibberish to him." Ox extinguished the final third of the stubby from hell in the ashtray perched on the armrest. He eye-pierced Tim for a few ticks and then tapped the pocket containing the envelope. "Good work, Mr. Phillips. My intel hunter-gatherer. My human surveillance camera. My eyes and ears among those who wish us tears."

"Chaff from the wheat. Rinse and repeat."

"You made it, son. You're now part of the Augustus O'Reilly Inner Circle. From now on, your words have ten times more weight. But!" Ox wiggled with his index finger. "With great power comes great headaches. So, use your heavily weighted words wisely."

"Yes, sir, I understand. And I thank you from the bottom of my soul." Tim touched his chest.

"Now." Ox stretched out in the armchair and clasped his hands on his chest. "Regarding Luke."

"I meant to ask, how are the parents doing?"

Luke was Markus and Lucy O'Reilly's first-born child, destined to inherit the top spot in the Magma energy empire. Augustus's daughter, Andrea, was next in the line of succession. With Luke's death, she became the ruler in waiting. But it was never that easy or clear cut when it came to deciding who would take the reins of the RED ORE® behemoth. The backstabbing was brutal; even the backroom deals were futile. There were too many moving parts for anyone to fully trust a supposed ally. Only an O'Reilly could get the top chair, but with such a large clan, there were a dozen plausible candidates.

"How are they doing?" Ox sighed. "Just imagine. You're Markus O'Reilly. King of the hill. Master of the known universe. You hold all the cards. Pull all the strings. Then one day your son is burned to death while standing in line for designer donuts."

Tim lowered his head. They sat in silence for a while.

"I know what you're thinking. 'Ox wants to use this mess to secure a spot on the throne for his daughter.' And yes, that's partially true. But if we don't build this fucking pipeline, the whole country's cooked."

"As soon as Kittay struck oil, I knew our carefree, soap-bubble-blowing days were numbered."

"At first everyone was happy. 'Oh look, they're investing in our real estate. Now we can finally buy even **more** crap.'"

"On the surface, it seemed like a win-win. But thinking folk like you and me knew better."

"Of course. We have more than half a brain." Ox thumb-pointed at the wet bar. "I'd offer you a drink, but we need clear heads tonight."

"Clear as crystal."

"Energy superiority was one of the few remaining advantages we had over Kittay. And now **they're** selling gas to **us?**"

"It's revolting."

"Even more than choco cigars." Ox sat up in the armchair, its leather crackling. "Our guys in the lab had been tinkering with a new synthetic fuel for ages, but Kittay striking oil lit a fire under their esteemed behinds. Have you seen the final numbers?"

"Yes, sir, just the other day. 'Magnificent' doesn't even touch it."

"But we need a new distribution system to spread the goodness. Trucks won't cut it. Not on the required scale."

"Hence the pipeline."

"And all the associated headaches, such as extortion from the landowners and legal minefields. Meanwhile, We Haul Gas® is more than happy to lap up cheap overseas oil and rake in the zalers. On the other hand, it's not like old El Presidente can call a news cruise and say, 'Everyone, please do as I say, or Kittay will throw us in chains.'"

"No, he can't. As soon as it's out there, it might become a self-fulfilling prophecy. Plus, it would look ultra-weak."

"Yeah, weaker than Brundell's chin. That's why we gotta hit 'em in their sleep, get crackin' on this fucking pipeline before the world knows how vital it is."

"Here's some gas up yer ass. Booyah!"

"Classy. And it's LRO, not gas."

"Classy, never again gassy."

"Your membership in the inner circle grants you a visit to the Augustus O'Reilly Chamber of Skeletons. There's a lever I pull and all—movie villain style. OK, it's not an actual lever. More like a longish button."

"Spooky."

"In this chamber, there's a map on the wall. Electronic map, on a screen. It shows the pipeline preparation progress. Green means go, red means no. You'll see for yourself. There are still a few red pockets, soon to be turned green either by hook or by crook." Ox sat back, his eyes misty from the memories. "I remember when the entire map was a sea of red. We were stuck around the northeastern tip of Herzland for a long time. Southern Norlandum too."

"Those tree humpers up there."

"If there's progress to be slowed, you can always count on them."

"That coxucker Kelski. Glad to see him banged up."

"The Cowherd's Pike guy? He enjoys blocking stuff. He better take the plea deal, or he'll be blocking cocks with his ass. Either way, we got that sector cleared."

"Funny how a seemingly unrelated prison escape aided our cause."

The VP smirked. "Did my counterintelli-man have his hand in the Kelski affair?"

"Does the Ox-man really want to know?"

"Back to the Luke situation. Even when that map is fully green, it won't mean squat unless RED ORE® can put its entire might behind the project. Politicos, media, business partners, investors, scientists, man on the street—all of them need to be singing the same tune. The one **we** wrote. But the company can't charge into battle when its leader is cooped up in a dark room, mourning his son and questioning the universe."

"Sucking his thumb?"

O'Reilly's mug turned purple.

"I apologize. I don't know what possessed me to say that."

The VP paused to de-fume. A minute ticked down.

"Tell me, Tim, how do we get our leader up and running again? How do we make him come back to the world that took so much from him?"

The aspiring puppet master dug his elbows into his thighs, planted his hands under his chin, and shut his eyes as he mulled it over.

"We gotta find the guy," he declared.

"The perp?"

"Yes, sir. You and me. Before the cops do."

"Have they released his name?"

Tim shook his head. "No. But I have an idea."

"Game face."

Patton Battaglia winked at his partner, Benji Gutierrez, as the Big Dog code flashed on his comm. He pressed a button. "Chief!"

Silence on the other end.

"Chief? Go for Battaglia."

"So? Do you have a name?"

"Not yet, sir. Zeroing in on a good-looking sus, though."

"Broadcastable?"

"Expecting confirmation or rejection within forty-eight."

"All we're gonna get is twenty-four before we're yanked to make room for the Ministry. They're already waiting in the wings, greasing their visors."

"I wondered what that smell was."

"Get me a solid name by tomorrow, Patton. I gotta throw a bone to those fucking leeches, give my poor bum a well-deserved rest."

"I feel you, Chief."

"Even lady politicos have sharpened their strap-ons and are ramming them in, sans lube."

"Ouch." Battaglia winced. "Permission to use United Vigilance?"

"Permission granted. We need every eye and ear we can get. By the way, you don't need to ask me for permission to use UV. You're the lead dog, so use whatever the fuck you need."

"Just wanted to make sure. This case is like no other."

Battaglia clicked off and swaggered toward Gutierrez, who was left- and right-swiping tips into "follow" or "forget" status.

"Anything to munch on?"

"I'd offer you a choco donut, but I fear getting slapped with a 'walking stereotype' tag by our ever-watchful free press."

Patton grinned. "How about a glazed one?"

"Yeah, glazed and confused. Like all of us." Benji head-pointed to a dozen Metro officers running headless chicken style thru the hastily assembled flamethrower case HQ. They had set it up in the basement of an auxiliary Metro building a few blocks away from the precinct because the media heat was starting to get in the way of the investigation. Literally. The decs had to wrestle the vultures just to get into the goddamn cop shop. Benji lost a jacket button, and Patton's chalk shirt got torn at the collar.

"Why did you tell him we've got a name when we've got zilch?" the junior dec asked.

"We may have zilch, but you know what **I've** got?" Patton flashed his black-ops comm and pressed a couple of buttons.

"Kerry? Battaglia."

"Dearest detective! How can United Vigilance assist you today?"

"You really have to ask?"

Kerry chuckled. "The flamethrower guy? Give me two days."

"I can give you one.

"Twenty-four hours and not a tick longer."

"Nuff chatting. Start hunting."

"Consider the hounds unleashed."

Battaglia switched off the comm. "Piece o' cake."

Benji shuddered. "UV will succeed where Metro has failed? Just put a slug in my skull already."

Battaglia glanced over his shoulder. "I'd take Kerry over ninety percent of these bums."

"You've got a point there."

"That cement mixer worker or whatever? Did anything come of that?" Battaglia poured himself a coffee. "Joe for Benji?"

"Nah, thanks. I gotta cut down. Turning into a black hole over here. The cement tip ended up in the same place as all the other ones—scrap heap of history." Benji pulled a squeezer on his mug. "I gotta catch some shut-eye."

"I still say this is extortion related. Gotta be."

"It's a prime-location QSR. The owner says they've got upstarting hoodlums trying their luck on a regular basis. Any one of them could have pulled this bone-header."

"They've got the lack of brains for it, for sure. But this wasn't a spur-of-the-moment thing—a guy gets drunk and hurls a bottle or something. This prick took the effort to put on a goddamn cosplay outfit. And where did he get that weapon?"

"Oh, this came in earlier." Benji tapped his comm screen. "AUAF 'has no records of any missing flamethrowers.' As if they'd notice something like that."

"Maybe he built it himself. DIY and watch 'em fry."

"You think he wanted there to be casualties? I mean, what was the target, the donut place or the people?"

"My money's on the donut place. But he misjudged the weapon's behavior."

"The finer points of flamethrowing, so to speak."

"Yeah. Talk about fickle." Battaglia dumped a coffee shot down his throat.

"Your thoughts?"

Tim Phillips presented the case for a vigilante solution to the Luke situation, then bated his breath as Ox O'Reilly weighed his decision.

Finally, the VP nodded. "Worth a shot."

"Nothing to lose. Except everything."

"And here I thought I'd be able to enjoy a game of pixkin in peace for once."

"No such luck, sir, I'm afraid. Vice-presidenting never sleeps."

"Exciting times, eh?" Ox slapped his palms together. "Disasters creating openings. The only question is how to squeeze thru and get a bigger piece of that pie in the sky. With all those around you being none the wiser."

"Phillips is the name, counter-intel is the game." Tim saluted. "They won't even know we were there."

"Like thieves in the night."

"Ain't that right."

"But first things first." The host turned to no one in particular. "Jenkins! Fetch my alternate-colors chariot. Posthaste!"

Tim's brow furrowed.

"There's no Jenkins," Ox clarified. "Or chariot. I just like the sound of it."

"Any news from the lab?" Battaglia asked his partner as he rummaged thru his desk's bottom drawer. "That piece of clothing they found."

"They were able to lift some usable stuff. It's possible it belonged to the killer, as none of the customers or donut people recognized it."

"By the time we get the results back, the roach'll be sipping spritzers on a distant beach. Or DIY-ing a bazooka in his garage. Now that he's gotten a taste for it."

"You wanna see the profiler's take?"

"Sure. We could all use a laugh." Battaglia burrowed even deeper into the drawer.

"What are you looking for?"

"Love. In all the wrong places." He grimaced as his arm reached its stretch limit. "Also, my Slix® Never Say Die™ puck."

"The what now?"

"My commemorative puck. Honoring their 2018 playoff run. You've seen it—black and red in a plastic cube."

"Oh, right! You keep it here? Not at the precinct?"

"You might have a point." Patton's mug un-frowned itself. "Nonetheless, it's a good thing I sent my hand drawer diving." He retrieved a 1/64-scale diecast Rampager® model. "Sporting its Tundra Thunder®-winning livery. From two years ago." His eyes glowed as he admired the mini monster truck.

Benji turned away from his screen. "Is something weird happening?"

"Gathering my meager possessions."

"Cop life no longer suits our brooding, grizzled hero?"

"Garbagemen for humans. That's all we are."

"Talk to me softly, why dontcha."

"This job is getting to me. The walls are closing in. Tarantulas digging at my eyelids. Wolves howling at the purple moon. Mars and Venus converging into an unholy alliance. My chest is bursting at the seams. So is my brain. Have you ever tasted a rainbow?"

"Sorry, sir, the 'real cop turned actor cop' auditions are one floor up."

Patton laughed and then reached for one of the Get It Twisted™ boxes on his desk. "Pretzel for a kingdom?"

"Those are good. Never tried them before yesterday."

"Catch."

The two men sat and munched in silence, occasionally glancing at their comms.

Battaglia finished his pretzel and a second coffee, then grabbed a napkin and de-crumbed his shirt. "I bet he no-sells it."

"Who? What?"

"Are you sitting down?"

Benji smiled and shrugged.

The veteran dec pushed a button on his official comm and waited. Moments later, he heard a click. "Chief? Battaglia. I realize my timing might be on the wonky side, but consider this my two weeks' notice. I deliver this prick and then ride off into the sunset."

"Less yapping. More hunting."

10 Furnace

"We have just learned that an evacuation order has been issued for the Farmer Dale's® area of Lower Herzland. Its residents woke up this morning to raging fires and smoke-covered skies. The cause? A WE HAUL GAS® fuel truck was making its delivery run during the night and crashed. The accident might have happened due to post-storm road conditions, but that hasn't been confirmed, as the firefighters are unable to reach the crash site at the heart of the inferno. 'Farmer Dale' Hofstetter himself was flying crop dusting rounds when he spotted the crashed truck and, suspecting thieves on the run, alerted the AUIM. Ministry officers were able to rescue the trapped driver and call in the local firefighters to secure the fuel truck. Unfortunately, by the time the fire crews reached the isolated location, the fires were already raging. Stay with us right here on Channel 5® for more on this developing story."

LIVE IN FAME—DIE IN FLAMES
WELCOME TO STAVENAGE SPEEDWAY®

Leo von Abzuger raised an eyebrow when his gaze met the (in)famous track motto. *There's no outcry to take this thing down?*

He parked his Divota® 600B™ in the team guest spot reserved for him, grabbed his windbreaker, and exited the car.

His cell phone rang. "Leo. Go."

"Man of the hour! Are you at the track?"

"Oh, it's you! Not your usual number?"

Neil Zorich chuckled. "Calling you from Da Louette.* The track has a little harbor, over by turn six."

Leo's knees buckled. "Your uncle's here?"

"As he stands and wheezes. Come join us."

Leo's stomach sank. "I thought we'd meet at your trailer."

"Change of plans."

Leo's voice broke. "Sure, no prob. Where do I go?"

"Where are you now?"

"Just passing the food stands."

"Stay put. I'm sending a drone to pick you up."

"Eh?"

"Lighten up, Leo! It's actually a guy in a golf cart."

"You've also got Zock Zimmer® lined up. We're looking to make inroads with non-traditional sports viewers ages eighteen to forty-five who intersect at gaming and action figures. We feel there's a goldmine just sitting there, untapped and unappreciated."

"What do they do? Zock whatever."

"You don't know? You're a legit zocker and you don't know?"

"The suspense is killing me."

"They spruce up people's gaming rooms."

"What, like hardware and shit?"

"Hardware and everything else. Chairs, accessories, lighting, sound, colors, toys, whatever the heart desires and their pockets can withstand."

Jimmy Lorenz's Told You So® liaison was machine-gunning him with sponsor and tie-in proposals over the phone while Buddy One was trying to get his attention from across the living room.

"Yeah, I guess we can tell them twenty . . ."

"Twenty what? Jimmy, are you OK? You don't seem your usual fully focused self."

Jimmy sat up on the couch. "Nah, it's just . . . some family drama might be brewing. Potentially."

"Rubber broke, girl's no joke?"

Jimmy chortled. "I wish."

"There'll always be some type of family drama no matter what. You've captured lightning in a bottle here. You don't wanna let moneymakers slip away due to sideshows."

"Sideshows are pretty much a given when your brother's a clown."

"Which makes him a sideshow clown. Score one for the numbers guy!"

"One."

"Any . . . um . . . any time frame for when the issue might get resolved?"

"Could you be any more greedy-corporate-typish? Soon! It must. One way or another."

"Big rivalry game coming up. Krantus will be looking to get revenge for the way they got embarrassed last time. People love the way you ridicule their 'strangling swarm' philosophy. Will your head be in it?"

"I'll turn it on for the game. I can go full charge for those few hours. Don't worry. You'll have your ridicule."

"Panning over to shaving products. Now, I know you said—"

"Mother of Mars, what is it already?! Sorry, yelling at Buddy One here. He's been giving me hand signals that only he understands for the past ten minutes."

"Can you remind him of Big Hat Bigger Cattle™?" Buddy One asked.

Brutus Nation 3   119

"The fuck is that?"

"The chips, remember? I was gonna go for my three-hour record."

"Buddy One is inquiring, as only he can, about those special-edition chips. Big Hat something."

"Big Hat Bigger Cattle™ by Kablamo Krunch®. What about it?"

"Are we featuring it? He wants to go for his chips-eating record."

"So far we've got Kablamo Krunch® Spec Edish penciled in for the trucks. But I can move the spot over to Big Hat if you want."

"Wait. They've got two separate special editions coming out?"

"They've got a **dozen** coming out. Keeps the buzz going."

"My concern is, isn't it too gimmicky? Too obvious? Buddy One going for the record, I mean."

"Borderline. How does he want to do it? I mean, he can't just reach for a shiny new chips bag that just happens to be lying there and go, 'I think I'm in the mood for some record-breaking munch action.'"

Knowing him, Jimmy thought. "How about this? Let's say halfway thru the third quarter someone says, 'Hey, Buddy, how many of these friggin' chips you've had so far?' Then everybody starts going back and forth on 'Buddy and the chips this' and 'Buddy and the chips that' until we realize he's close to his old record. Well, **current** record. Then we start rooting for him. 'Kill— the—chips! Fill—a—ditch!' I'll work on the rhymes."

"**Now** you're cookin'."

"Isn't that Feed the Feast®?"

"It is. It felt right to say it, even though they're not a sponsor. Too mainstream for us. Lacks that edge."

"Yeah. Edge is where **this** beast goes to feast." Jimmy thumped his chest.

"How about this one, then? A punch-packing pretzel chain exploding in popularity."

"The beast is all ears."

"Where is greatness forged?" Ox asked.

"In the fiery dungeons of hell," the King replied.

"Let the descent begin!"

Augustus O'Reilly heel-turned and exited the King of All Engineer's command center at Muskeg Facility West. The King and Timothy Phillips followed him out of the room.

The three men took a kidney-jiggling industrial elevator ride into the proverbial guts of the facility. Cranks rattled, pipes snaked, hydraulics hammered, drills whined, barrels rolled, metal clanged, steam hissed, and heat blissed.

They reached a machine lovingly referred to as a cauldron and stopped. Sprinkled thruout the plant, the giant stubby titanium bins served as mega energy processors, pumping power into Athenia's veins. Even as they stood a hundred feet away, they felt the cauldron's scorching heat walloping their skin.

The King of All Engineers felt obliged to impart a health warning. "Augustus, sir, we really shouldn't be standing—"

O'Reilly finger-shot Tim, who grabbed the King at the elbow and knee-to-legged him down to the floor.

Ox took a step closer and loomed over the King. A minute passed, and no one spoke. The King knew there was nobody within a 300-meter radius. In fact, he **preferred** the nighttime solace.

Ox reached into his RED ORE® winter jacket pocket and held his hand there. *This seems like a good time to start panicking.*

Just as the King was about to break the suffocating silence, Ox flashed a piece of paper. He stepped toward the engineer as he read from the sheet. "And I quote, 'While Liquified Red Ore shows staggering potential as a domestically sourced and processed energy solution of tomorrow, the byproducts and possible negative side effects of its usage are yet to be properly explored and evaluated. As such, I am currently of the opinion that LRO's overall impact, both on people and the environment, should be analyzed further before it is granted the government's seal of approval.'"

"Ox, I had no choice! It's the government!"

"I wasn't finished!"

Another stretch of silence. Except for the machinery.

"End quote." Ox crumpled up the paper and threw it at the King's head. "There's your fucking crown, you piece of human garbage."

"It's the government! **The government!**" King tried getting up, but Tim pushed him back down and pressed his boots on his calves.

O'Reilly lunged forward, grabbed the King by the jaw, and venom-spit into his mug. "Do you not realize what's at stake here, you momo to end all momos?! The company! **The country!** All we hold dear! The right way, the golden day! What our fathers bled for and our mothers wept for! It's not bad enough we got We Haul Gas® on our ass, we also gotta waste time smoking out snakes in our own goddamn yard?!" Ox pushed the King's head away, then turned his back to him and stepped away.

"Ox, please! The board came to me with death in their eyes! I had to tell the truth!"

The VP was silent.

"I did say LRO is the future. Just not the present. We need more time."

When O'Reilly finally spoke again, his voice was low. "With each passing day, Kittay is fucking us deeper in the ass with their cheap gas. We're talking almost loss-leader prices. They laid the bait, and the country got hooked. Time, my king without a crown, has run out."

"I was gonna tell Tim about the Board, I swear! Just the other day I was havering. Rock or a hard place? Some choice."

"Why should I believe you? You'll say anything at this point."

"Ask Lexi! She'll vouch."

Ox still had his back turned to the King. "Lexi? From Insulation? The one Tim's been shtupping?"

"You knew about that, sir?" Phillips stammered.

"No. Until now." Ox turned to the King. "She knew about this?"

"Not the specifics, only that something was weighing on me. She suggested I come clean no matter what it was."

Ox turned back around and approached the King. He grabbed his jaw, pulled him closer, and stared into his soul. "Magma, c'est moi." He turned to Tim: "String him up!"

"We are now live at the scene with Dale Hofstetter, the owner of agricultural giant Farmer Dale's®." Lin Wesley turned to the digital pop-up on her right, where a drained face was looking into the camera.

"Farmer Dale, we've seen the images and heard the sounds. You're obviously in the thick of it. What's the situation on the ground?"

"Hi, Lin! I hope you and the world can hear the urgency in this tired old farmhand's voice. We're up a translucent creek with not a single goddamn paddle in sight. And even the bloody boat is leakin' like a sieve."

"Can you give us more details on how the fire started and how it spread so quickly?"

"There I was, flying my little crop duster, givin' the business to the critters. Allasudden, I spotted a crashed truck. At first I figured it was rustlers, so I called the Ministry. Then I saw a GD fireball startin' to puff. Turned out it was a gas truck on a night run. Crashed like a pro, all over my green babies."

"Those would be your plants, I assume."

Farmer Dale got distracted by something outside of the shot, then refocused his attention on the lens. "Yes, ma'am, my trees and veggies. Nuts but never saggies."

Did he just wink at me? "Now, regarding the evacuation order. What has the response been like? Are the people leaving their homes, as instructed?"

"Yes, but we need to pick up the pace. This fire? I ain't seen nothing like it. The speed is . . . bewildering."

"Any word on when it might be reined in? What's the fire department telling you?"

Dale paused and looked past the camera. "Zoom out, son."

The camera panned out to reveal Hofstetter sporting a firefighter uniform. "Sure, we've got fellas from all over the union coming in to lend a hand, but Farmer Dale is still the chief protector of these here lands. Fire, blaze, flame, no matter the name, Dale's got game."

"Sir, we've heard—"

"Sorry, Lin, time to get back in the fight." The farmer zipped up the thick jacket. "Keep your eye on Channel 5®!"

Leo von Abzuger stepped onto the deck of *Da Louette*. He couldn't hear or see anyone, so he turned around to ask the golf cart driver where to go, but the man had already whirred away.

Leo descended into the lavish salon as marble glistened and crystal glinted. "Um . . . Neil? It's me, Leo! I'm here."

"We're down here!"

"Neil? It's Leo!"

"I know, for fuck's sake! We're one floor down!"

Leo walked down another flight of stairs until he reached the two Zorich men, each wearing swimming trunks and lying on a Scowling Owls®-branded inflatable pool floatie.

"Give the poor mare some time. She just lost a possible hubby-to-be. I can't be all 'here's **my** penis now, whaddaya think?'" Neil nabbed a peach from a fruit tray next to him.

Lou finger-wiggled. "But not **too much** time! Don't sleep on it. There'll be a mess of penises bivouacked around her castle within a week. You know how they are."

"Penises? Yes, they really are the worst."

Lou laughed. "Remember, you have the inside track. You literally saved her ass. It's only right for you to claim it."

Neil looked at Leo and thumb-pointed at his uncle. "Lou Zorich, the hopeless romantic."

"Whaddaya think?" Lou kneaded his enormo-gut, proudly displaying it for Leo. "Sexiest belly dancer in all the land?"

Leo gulped. "I . . . I like it."

"Would you look at him? White as a ghost, shivering while shaking. He still thinks I might kill him."

Neil chuckled. "That true, Leo? You think I invited you here so my uncle could strangle you?"

Leo shrugged.

"On his own boat? I hope you realize there are better ways for billionaires to off a fool."

"Yes. But **this** billionaire likes his puppeteering. And garroting."

The Zoriches laughed. Neil pointed to an owl-shaped pool floatie. "Grab a pew and sit for a few."

Leo sat down on the floatie. *Comfier than it looks.*

"Speaking of billionaires," Neil said as he cut a chunk of pineapple from the fruit tray, "are you on your way?"

"On my way? To billionaire status? If I live to be five hundred."

"Awww, no need for false modesty. Your pretzels are on everyone's tongue. Literally."

"Sounds like something Mad Dog* would say."

"Did you hear? He's hanging up the wheel after this season."

"Finally."

"No love for the rabid puppy?"

"I used to love his antics back in the day, but enough already. He's hangin' on like a cobra on a zebra."

"He's skint. Needs the moolah."

"Busted marriage?"

"Multiple."

"Good thing my wife has her own money. The only reason she was available was on account of her ex being sent up the river."

"Who owns the company? The two of you, jointly?"

Leo shook his head. "I launched Get It Twisted™ shortly before I met her. There are partners and investors, including Beli, but I have the biggest share and the final say."

"Good. Keep it that way. Coz there's an IPO just around the corner."

"As in going public?"

"Yes."

"Good to know. Since, you know, I'm the owner and all that."

"Hey, didn't you say you'd bring a baker's bag or something?"

"A Baker Bunker Bag™, yes. We're very proud of those. I've got a few in the car. Should I go get them? I didn't wanna lug 'em across the track—"

"Do you know who your pretzels have to thank for their sudden surge in popularity?"

Leo's mug dropped. "Don't tell me."

Neil grinned and nodded.

"Uncle Lou?"

"Unkie Lou and his heart of gold." Neil nodded at Lou, who seemed to be inspecting his belly for potential imperfections. "He arranged it with the guvner."

"All that just to raise a pretzel chain's profile?"

"Are you being a momo again? They did it to knock out Old Man Kelski and make room for the pipeline. The pretzel truck was a happy bonus. Oh, before I forget, we're bringing in Mad Dog's nephew next year to take his place. Get It Twisted™ will sponsor his ride."

"Cool." Leo shrugged. "We likely would have folded without the bust-out boost."

"Folded like so many pretzels."

"Haaaa."

"So," Neil squeezed out the pit from a plum, "tomorrow, we'll front you a few million, and you'll start buying up Aurelian Grade C agricultural land."

"I will?"

"Yes. In the past, developing Grade C land made no economic sense. But now that Lower Herzland is on fire . . ." Neil glanced at Lou, who nodded.

"Grade C looks mighty fine to me."

"Margins will be lower, so food prices will climb higher," Neil continued. "But expensive food is better than no food at all. The law says only food-producing companies are allowed to buy that type of land. And they must show actual food products stemming from the land within two years of purchase. Thus, there are no pesky hedge funds to outbid. Keeps the price per hectare at a tolerable level. As a food maker suddenly aflush with cash, Get It Twisted™ is in prime position to grab those acres. Lou and I will get our ROI when the company goes public, and all that lovely investor money starts rolling in."

"Is my head supposed to be spinning? Coz it definitely is."

Neil finished off the plum. "You can't stop progress."

Jimmy Lorenz was laid out on his living room couch, his eyelids heavy from a lack of sleep and his mind racing with worry and sponsor proposals.

"Whaddaya say?"

Jimmy one-eyed Buddy One, who had been droning on about chip-eating strategies for the past ten minutes. "Huh?"

"About the dip."

"Dip?"

"What kind of dip should I go with? Mild or savory? Chunky or smooth? Maybe no dip at all? Would leave more room in the old tummy."

"Where's a sniper when you need one?"

"Why so nasty? These are legit tactical concerns. The chip battlefield is hotly contested. No margin for error. One wrong move and pop goes the dream."

"The dream of chip-eating glory is one we should all aspire to, I grant you, but I've got things on my mind."

Buddy pulled a concerno-mug. "Care to share?"

"This ain't daytime TV, Buddy Zero One. Real men sob silently in their cave. Speaking of which, what happened with the AbsorBlow® figure you were gonna offer as a gift to the bobblehead gods?"

Buddy smacked his forehead. "Total forgottence."

"And **you** wanna break chip-gorger records?"

"Well, my **own,** yes."

"We've got a nice display over there, but a toy room without AbsorBlow® . . . that's just laziness."

"Next time you see me, if I ain't toting good sir AbsorBlow®, throw me out of the house. Better yet, don't even let me in. Frontier justice!"

"Seems like throwing you out on your ass would be a harsher punishment than turning you away. We'll see which mood strikes."

"A tough but fair ruler. We salute you."

Jimmy's Earwig® buzzed. "Lucky Junior! Pleasure or pain?"

"Hey, Jimmy. Any word on Tommy?"

"Not a peep. You?"

"Nah. But I'm hearing stuff thru the old grapevine."

"What is it?"

"Can . . . um . . . can you talk freely?"

Jimmy turned to Buddy. "We're done here, dawg. See you tonight for the game." Then he spoke into the phone. "Sure."

"Do you know who Crowbar Kerry is?"

Jimmy stalled until he heard the door close behind Buddy One. "Street guy. Living legend. Cross him and you will kneel before his balls of steel."

"Yeah, he's with UV now. I hear he's joined the hunt for the flamethrower guy."

Jimmy sling-shotted off the couch. "Mother of Mars."

"Time is ticking even faster now. We gotta find Tommy before Kerry does."

"And who will run those tests?"

"**I** will! I'll tell them we ran more tests, and now we can confirm LRO is safe. Please, Ox, you don't need to do this!"

Ox had been yelling at the King for the past fifteen minutes, complete with a purple mug and a foaming mouth. Tim had hooked up the engineer to a piece of machinery that was normally used to deliver parts and tools to repairmen thruout the plant. The King was hanging from a strap tied up like a harness, his legs dangling above a ragged chasm. Add to that the heat from the cauldron, which was getting unbearable even for Tim, who was standing farthest away from it.

"You already told them you think it's unsafe!"

"I said **'currently!'** I '**currently**' think it might be unsafe before further tests! I left myself wiggle room."

"Yeah? So now what, you ran more tests that miraculously proved that the substance is perfectly safe? Not even the Board is dumb enough to buy that!"

"I can sell it! I can sell it to them! **Please!**"

Ox approached the safety railing with a grim expression. He grabbed it with both hands as his shoulders slumped. His eyes closed, he stood there for a few minutes.

"Bring him back."

Tim pressed a button on the wall, and the giant toolbox whirred back to safety.

"What's next for the King, sir?"

"We'll need to beef up all this stuff—the pipes, the cauldrons, the pumps. Build a whole new network across the country. We'll need the King for that. Cheap gas from Kittay? So those bastards wind up buying every inch of our land? Not while **this** ticker is ticking." Ox thumped his chest and dropped a loogie down into the chasm. "Motherfuckers."

Tim waited until the VP's mug de-purpleized.

"Just to cement it, sir, you decided to spare the ax for good? We won't drop it down the road?"

"He's our best and brightest. You can't kill everybody."

11 Lava®

Kerry Douglas pulled up to the White Wizard's mansion and jumped out of his United Vigilance SherzKex®.

He walked up the driveway and was buzzed in without ringing the bell. Passing by the front lawn, he nodded at the garden crews who were pampering hedges and trimming edges.

When he reached the pool area, he smiled at the sight of Titbuster Toni's giant chrome dome gleaming in the sunlight. Then he spotted the Wizard prepping a grill and waved at him. "Carping the old diem?"

"Hey, Kerry! Good to see ya. I'm pretending I know how to work this thing. Trying to impress my . . . guest."

Buster was sitting on a white plastic chair, his eyes semi-closed and his body drenched in sweat. Next to him was a half-empty jar of Red Widow Peppers®.

Looks like he's steeling himself for another round of heat from hell.

"How's it going so far?" Kerry took off his LazerWraptor® shades and shook the Wizard's hand.

"Like sharing a bunk with a gorilla."

"There are worse things."

"Oh?"

"Sharing a bunk with a **horny** gorilla."

The host took a swig of his short drink. "Counting my blessings. How . . . um . . . how does it reflect . . . how does it manifest . . ."

Kerry grinned. "No way around it. Your bathroom will soon curse the day it was born."

"Good to know. I'll issue the biohazard protocol order to my crew."

"You should. We're talking chemical warfare levels here."

"Mother of Gawd," the host murmured into his glass. "Would you look at all that sweat. Where does **that** go?"

"Here, watch this." Kerry called out to Buster. "Yo, Toni, show the Wizard how you towel off!"

The perspiring hulk rose from his chair, planted his feet, struck a pose, and pulled a human version of the doggie head-to-toe dry-off. Sweat shrapnel came flying off his enormous head and shoulders, besmirching several poolside accessories.

Those are bound for the backyard incinerator as soon as I get rid of these two pests, the Wizard thought. *If I ever do.*

Kerry slapped the Wizard's upper arm. "I keep telling him he should upload this shit to Told You So®, start selling tickets. Get a tour going. People would pay to watch."

The dentist forced a smile, then took two gulps of his drink.

"What say we give our tired old pegs a break?" Kerry pointed to the set of poolside furniture.

"Oh, sure, sure," the Wizard replied. "Would you like some iced tea? Whiskey?"

"No thanks. I keep a giant bottle of CherryBlast® ReCharge in my car. Keeps me hydrated as I drive."

Once comfortably slumped on a shaded chaise lounge, Kerry placed his LazerWraptors on a wicker table between him and the Wizard. "How's the first installment looking?"

The Wizard shook his head. "Grim."

"Are those trucks to blame?" When pulling up to the house, Kerry had noticed a trio of delivery trucks parked next to the main gate.

"Not the trucks. The cargo."

"What is it?"

"Truck number one, new furniture. Second overhaul this year. Truck number two, terrarium equipment. If you're wondering what that is, that makes two of us."

"Truck number three?"

"Shoes."

Crowbar paused to watch Buster ingest two more peppers, adding a further layer of sweat.

"Do you plan on gambling again?"

"It's my only joy. As soon as I get you the money, I'll be back in black. Get my revenge on Battaglia."

"Fat chance of seeing **him** again. After he's done cracking this latest case, I hear he'll split for Las Islas and spend the rest of his days under a palm tree perfecting his hammock-lounging techniques."

"All on **my** dime. Lucky bastard."

"Tell Uncle Kerry what's really going on here. Why are you so strapped?"

"Aside from what I mentioned after the card game?"

"Golf court, chefs, mansions, multiple hush monies, and so forth."

"Here's the skinny. My kids are good eggs. Considering the spoilerama I dropped on their heads, they're surprisingly well-balanced and smart. One is doctorizing at Stavenage. Another one is slaying it in the DREQ® futures. The younger ones are all at walled-off schools and pre-schools. They have so many recitals, I'm looking at actor headshots, trying to find a double to take my place at those fucking hellscapes."

The Crowbar belly-laughed.

"But the one thing they're not is athletic. Neither was I, to be clear. I took one at-bat in Lickle League® and fouled off the ball. It hit my foot and bounced up, smacking me right in the hooter. I wound up in the ER." The Wizard pointed at his mug. Kerry leaned in and winced at the sight of a crisscross of faded scars.

"The way I see it, I've got one major goal to go: to produce an athlete. My fiancé's family is loaded with spartan-type wunderkids. Her—"

"Wunder**kinds**," Titbuster interjected from where he sat and sweated.

Kerry and Wizard exchanged perplexed looks. Buster said no more, so the Wizard continued. "Her dad and uncle, they both played Higher 10 baseball. The uncle won the title with the Porcupines®. Her mom starred at North Magma in lacrosse. The Spendosaurus Rex herself? I met her down in Las Islas. She was cliff diving and mid-air spinning. I had to turn over onto my front to hide my hard-on. All these reasons make her the spot-on wife number three candidate."

"Those off-the-books kids you mentioned the other day, no spartan genes there?"

"Too early to tell." The Wizard finished his drink. "Even if they **do** have a knack for it, who knows when or if I'll be able to pull the 'proud father beaming with pride' gimmick at their games?" He lowered his voice. "And if my fiancé found out I've blundered two secret boogers in the time I've known her . . ."

"Spartan fury?"

"I'd have to run for my life. I ain't even joking. I think she'd kick my ass in a fight. Or at least go down in flames."

Kerry head-pointed toward the delivery trucks. "The semis full of financial quicksand? Just the price of doing business?"

"Yep. Getting a prime-stock woman of child-bearing age to hitch her star to an old fart like me? That's a tall order no matter what the color of my wizard robe is."

"To hitch her **wagon** to an old fart's **star**," Toni said, volunteering another edit.

"Getting a taste for public speaking, there, Buster?"

The big man burped, then swallowed another handful of hotties and patted his belly. "Prepping for the eruption."

Kerry smiled and stretched, cracking his elbows. "If you can't even come up with the first installment, o whitest of all wizards . . ." He got up from the chaise lounge and put his LazerWraptors back on. "Then the time has come for the two of us to have a one-on-one heart-to-heart. My car."

Crowbar headed down the driveway toward his UV SherzKex®. The White Wizard followed suit, his snout hanging low.

"'Fires of hell.' I get it." Hugo Jimenez pointed at the curtain of smoke rising from the refinery towers crowding the sky behind the stadium.

"I knew you would." Esteban Estez unbuckled his seat belt as his chopper touched down at RED ORE® Field, the proud home of Magma Lava®.

The viscount and the lawyer got out and rushed across the helipad into the owner's suite-bound elevator. Their ears were still recovering from the helo's audio assault when the elevator reached its destination, and the doors opened.

"And this little piggy went to the end zooooone!" Timothy Phillips greeted them with a wide grin and a short drink in each hand.

Estez smiled. "Never get tired of that one."

"Practicing for a game show host gig, Tim?" Jimenez asked.

Estez frowned. "Aren't you supposed to be mourning Luke?"

Tim pulled a quick 360, then lowered his voice. "Who's gonna know? The others are still downstairs, mugging for the cameras. Stop scaring me like that, Your Excellency."

"By 'others,' I assume you mean the usual Ox entourage?"

"That is correct, counselor. Only more somber than usual, obviously." Tim handed the drinks to the two guests.

The viscount took a sip. "Is she here?"

Tim nodded. "In all her glory."

"If I was twenty years younger . . ." Hugo swirled his drink.

"You'd **still** have no shot. But you'll always have **my** love. How's that?"

"I'll take it." The lawyer clinked the viscount's glass and then took a swig.

"Gentlemen!" Augustus O'Reilly entered the suite and shook hands all around. "Big night. Lava® hasn't been in the playoff mix this late in the season for years."

Although a storied franchise with a rabid following, Lava® was riding a fifteen-year playoff drought. Their most recent championship had come in 1983 when they outgrinded the Filibusters® in a 10–7 snoozathon.

"Hmm . . ."

"What's wrong, Esteban?"

"Now that I see you two standing next to each other, are you tanning buddies?"

Ox and Tim looked at each other, then fell down laughing.

"That's the first time I've laughed since we lost Luke." Ox grabbed a paper towel from the kitchenette and wiped his eyes. "What can I tell you, Esteban? We're in a tough business. Me and ol' Tim, we had to go down to the Furnace, sort out a loose screw."

"Say no more." The viscount raised his glass, then downed it.

"Um, say, Esteban, when the others arrive, we won't be able to talk in any meaningful way. Care to join me in the next room for a brief chat?"

"One tiny room, two living legends."

They stepped into the office adjoining the suite's main room.

"I need to sound you out on a delicate matter."

"What else are luxury boxes for?"

"It's actually Tim's idea. If you shoot it down, he gets the blame."

"What are security officers for?"

"Heh." Ox gazed out the window at the ever-smoggy Muskeg night. "This lunatic who killed Luke, we want the fucker. We **need** the fucker. For our own sanity's sake. For our own **legacy's** sake." He paused. "Perhaps the viscount can assist?"

"The O'Reilly reach doesn't extend to AC?"

"Not for something like this. Not on such short notice. Putting on a hunting party in a matter of hours? My guys know Magma—every nook and brook. But they have no clue under which rock a roach might be hiding in AC."

Estez was silent for a minute. "Every cop in AC is looking for him. Getting to him before any of **them** do? That's a tall order."

"**How** tall?"

Estez mulled it over. Looking out the window, his eye caught a stack of smoke billowing from one of the power plants. "This new pipeline coming up, how close to reality is it?"

"**Very** close. Looking to break ground before the year is out."

"Can you send a—I'm sure there's a technical term for it—a main line my way?"

"Yorba Woods?" Augustus shrugged. "We can send the pipes practically anywhere. The only question is time and cost. You want **more** pipeline construction than necessary in your region?"

"No, not in a vacuum. But see, I've been tug-o-waring with Harrington over taxes for five months already. One inch here, one inch there, but no breakthru yet. If I had a strategically vital hose in my pocket, I might be able to leverage it into milk and honey."

"I'm a funds and bonds man myself."

"That works too."

"If we give you a key line, you'll quash the roach for us?"

Estez looked at Ox and nodded.

"Done." They shook on it.

"Soon as I'm done with my Lin Wesley interview, I'm making the roach my top priority. As a bonus, I'll put the fear of Mars into her, make her charm the Herzland into falling in love with the pipeline."

Ox's eyes doubled in size. "You can do that?"

"To get the CG's grubby hand out of my people's pockets? With gusto."

The viscount rushed for the door. Before opening it, he turned back to O'Reilly. "The Hogs® have clinched the playoffs, and Lava® is on the bubble. Want me to call down to Coach Bez and ask him to take the foot off the pedal tonight?"

"I **am** tempted, but no. Let's keep it to one cunning plan per meeting."

Jimmy Lorenz was guzzling Mocha Muchachos® and frenzy-dialing every known acquaintance Tommy ever had, going all the way back to kindergarten. He reached a lot of them, but none of them had seen or heard from Tommy in the past few days.

He had PigzNet® running on mute, trying to one-eye the build-up to that night's college revenge clash. Trying but not succeeding. *How could anyone focus under such circumstances? Just as WUWI started to gain serious sponsor steam. What was that momo thinking?!*

Jimmy jumped up from the couch but got woozy and had to sit back down. *I gotta get some fresh air. This is unbearable. On three. One, two . . .*

He rose to his feet and unmuted PigzNet®. *Let it be background noise while I'm getting ready.*

He entered the hallway and flicked on the light. *Is that a headlight in the driveway?* He glanced thru the front-door window into the descending darkness but saw no car other than his own. *I must've been thrown off by the hallway light. Bloody tricks of the racing mind.*

He put on a pair of thick-soled boots and reached for a FreezeKill® jacket. A bang on the door made him drop the jacket and bounce off a wall.

Two more wake-the-dead bangs were followed by continuous doorbelling. Jimmy was close to fainting.

He peeked thru the window and was strangely relieved to see a UV badge. He opened the door as his heart deaccelerated.

Kerry Douglas stepped inside. "Pick up your jacket, Jimmy! We're taking a trip to Nudwick."

Esteban Estez sat chit-chatting opposite Lin Wesley in one of the RED ORE® Field media rooms. Aside from Lin's crew, no one else was around.

Once the crew was out of the earshot, Lin leaned in. "Why did you agree to this outrageous fee? Why did it have to be me and no one else?"

"I wanted to find out what your price is for an unearned interview. And now I know."

"Impressed?"

"The balls on you!" Estez grinned. "And yes. I thought you'd agree four offers ago."

"But why me?"

"You've got them hooked. The Herzland. They hang on your every word. I've never seen anything like it. I expect you to be an asset for years to come. The upcoming pipeline and such. Our golden sparrow. Our queen of hearts and minds. You know what they say: Whoever controls Herzland . . ."

"Controls Athenia."

Esteban nodded.

"I don't write the words. I only deliver them. And with all due respect, why does the viscount of Yorba Woods care about the hearts and minds of Herzland?"

"I control the entire Channel 5® media family. Top to bottom. The words will be whatever I want them to be. You just need to deliver them with the trademark goose-pimple-inducing Lin Wesley conviction. Yorba and Herzland . . . the pipeline will bring us together."

"I assume I won't be paid for this interview?"

"Oh, yes, ma'am, you will. A deal's a deal. Speaking of which, your contract is up in a year. I'm thinking a hundred percent raise. Or you can walk out that door and start your own Told You So® channel."

"Why not tell me about all this as a prerequisite of hiring me?"

"Impossible to know whether you'd be a hit. The audience decides that, not me."

Lin nodded as she absorbed the info. "Devil in the details, eh?"

"Sorry?"

"Never mind. You can consider me a proud asset of the Channel 5® family." She sat back in her chair and called out to the crew. "Guys, are we ready?"

"Soft lobs only, please."

"As you wish, Your Excellency."

12 Slayer

"Son-in-law number five, fill my good ear with some good news."

"Wish I could, father-in-law number one. We got fires licking skies like horny hounds from hell, complete with the devil grinning and shitting."

"Will the devil ever learn good manners, fix my quandary?"

"That's a chop with a hop on the devil amending his devilish ways, Savior Dale. I . . . I think our mother farm is done for."

"We'll rebuild. We always have, whether winds from heaven or hounds from hell."

"Thought you were all googly on deserting these here lands. Or was that a different Dale bending my ear?"

Randy Hendricks was sit-repping Dale Hofstetter over Earwig® as their world was imploding in smoke. Randy had just wrapped up the evac effort in his designated section of the land.

"**You** will," Farmer Dale said after a pause. "Rebuild, that is. The young folk need a leader like you."

"Where's a hankie when you need it?"

"Fire must have gotten it."

"CG says they're sending more fire crews. You want me to suit up too?"

"Negative. I need you on livestock duty, save as many as you can. Get 'em into trains at Sector D. We're running non-stoppers over into Aurelia."

"Roger. Heading there now."

"Stay solid, son-in-law."

"What's in Nudwick?"

"Industrial scenery. Plus a roach."

Kerry Douglas sat at the wheel of his UV SherzKex® with Jimmy Lorenz riding shotgun. The night was chilly, the traffic sparse. The moon? Obscured behind a cover of clouds.

"The roach's name wouldn't happen to be Thomas Lorenz, would it?"

Crowbar nodded.

"You want me to help bring him in?"

"The O'Reillys want to see a body, dead or alive. The sooner the better. Otherwise, they'll go on a warpath, make life miserable for all kinds of people, whether they're connected to Luke's death or not."

Jimmy looked to his right, gazing at AC burbs in silence. "Is this car... um... wired?"

"Negative." Kery paused. "What's pressing on your soul?"

"I ain't killing my brother. You can tie me to a rack, you can hang, drown and/or quarter me, you can threaten to off my pops—"

"Whoa, Jimmy!" Kerry seemed genuinely shocked and amused. "This ain't Rick Wrecker®.[13] UV is a proud part of the law enforcement community. People who are reluctant to talk to cops? They come to us. We can go where the official boot cannot."

"Opening doors and cuddling whores."

"Um... okay."

---

13 Rick Wrecker®: A smash hit TV series that ran from 1980 thru 1988. The titular character was a disillusioned ex-cop who, aided by his talking toilet sidekick Bowly®, stalked the streets in search of scum. "Wreck Mode" T-shirts are bestsellers to this day.

"How does dead-or-aliving my brother mesh with enforcing the old law?"

"I hear you. I'd be asking the same question if I were in your shoes. But I also submit to you that the alternative is much worse. For everyone involved."

"Alternative?"

"The O'Reilly wrath." Kerry glanced at the WUWI star. "Surely, none of us want to see how **that** would mesh with stuff."

Jimmy slumped deeper in the seat as a carbon-colored cloud darkened his mug.

Farmer Dale broke free of the anaconda of a fireman's suit and slumped down on a couch in the Farmer Dale's® airstrip hangar office. He was instantly reminded of what a stretch it was to call that thing a "couch." After forty-odd years of existence, it was more like a hardened lump of foam blown up to couch proportions by alien weapon tech.

He shut his eyes and exhaled like what he imagined ancient titans did. Post-world-building type of huff level. The fight against the fire was lost, at least as far as Dale's crew was concerned. Might as well join their families in safety. Nothing further they could do there. The professionals had started pouring in. Let them have a go at it.

He was happy with how the evac had gone down. So far no casualties had been reported. The Hofstetter clan was on their way to relatives, mostly in Upper Herzland. Some in Aurelia and Magma. Dale planned on hopping a plane out of there—his own. There was still a smoke-free corridor he could fly thru.

I better get on with it.

He rolled off the lump of a couch, dragged himself to the tiny bathroom, and took a shower that felt so good it should have been illegal. He deployed a dozen generous pumps of Pamper Me Gently® Clean+Serene™ For Men CharcoalCharge™ gel, rinsed out his hair with a sandalwood-smelling shampoo, splashed a double-hand of mouthwash on his teeth (no strength left for toothbrushing), and stepped out of the bathroom smelling like a rose but still feeling drained like a prune.

He decided a two-hour sleep was the way to go. Any less and he'd be in no shape to fly. Any more and the smoke-free corridor might be gone for good.

Lemme grab the digi-watch in the office to set the alarm. There's also a sleeping bag in there. Better than the ruddy couch.

He entered the office and jumped at the sight of Randy Hendricks, son-in-law number five, sitting grim-faced behind the desk.

"Hiya, Dale."

Cynthia Lennox ex-Holman was leafing thru the latest issue of *DiamondBlack® Magazine*, her tastes growing more refined by the minute. The copy had been given to her by Hugo Jimenez as an incentive to get the CG deal done. "Sew up the seams and realize your dreams," he had said. The CGR had proven a hard nut to crack, but Cynthia finally had the 800-pound gorilla piece on the chessboard. *Ooh, a yacht featuring a fully functioning Bowly® replica! Damned if I'll let a CGR stand between me and old Bowly®!*

Up until a few years ago, she had been steadily upwardly mobiling when her then-husband decided to bet the proverbial farm and blow up their lives.* After ditching the momo and keeping the kids, she reinvented herself as viscount Esteban's chief Harrington lobbyist. She had managed to win a few minor battles thus far, but tonight could be the night she won the war.

She turned the page. *Is that a castle? Yep, sure as flies flock to shit, they up and built a medieval-type castle on a private island in Las Islas. Fully functioning drawbridge! Naturally.*

Her Earwig® buzzed. She got up from the hotel bed, exhaled yoga-style, closed her eyes, and answered the phone. "Thanks so much for getting back to me, CGR. I know you—"

"Cynthia, you know I love you, but we're up to our necks in refugees. Unless you really, **really** have the magic bullet, please don't call me until next month."

"But I **do** have it. The magic bullet."

"Eh? Are you **sure**? Please don't tease me."

"Regarding the refugees. Yorba Woods can help."

WELCOME TO EAST NUDWICK
PROUD HOME OF THE FEARSOME PORCUPINES®

"Hey, didja catch the sign?" Kerry pointed at the Board as they drove by. "Wouldn't you know it? I talked to a guy today who's engaged to a girl whose uncle was on the championship team. What are the odds?"

"Which one?"

"Which sign?"

"No, which championship team? They won a few."

"Aw, man, I never asked. You really know your sports, eh?"

"It's my life. Ever since I was a tiny tot. And now I finally have a way to make money with it."

"I assume your dad used to take you to games."

"That he did. My mom too, actually. Especially baseball." Jimmy smiled. "Those were the days."

"The golden days of carefree childhood. Too bad we had to grow up."

"I'm still clinging to it. Ever see my Doomers collection?"

Crowbar laughed. "I ain't a subscriber, I admit, but I checked out your brand once we got on Tommy's trail. Quite a display."

"It'd be ten times smaller without my WUWI dough. Streaming was my savior."

"Sweet gig."

"It makes me shine."

A message flashed on the car's UV comm.

"They want me to turn on the civvy radio. Something pertinent." Kerry hit a button, and a radio station came on:

"Police in Athenia City now believe they have a prime suspect in the Donuts or Nothing® attack that left one dead and four wounded. Thomas 'Tommy Lo' Lorenz, a reputed gangland figure, is said to have been involved in extortion attempts on the store. At this time, we can only speculate about his motive, but the authorities see it as a possible act of intimidation or revenge against the owners. Tommy Lorenz's whereabouts are unknown. If you have any information regarding his location, please contact the police immediately."

Crowbar turned the radio down and looked at Jimmy. "You'll thank me later."

"For what?"

"For getting you out of your house."

"What do you mean?"

"Your brother has just been turned into the country's numero uno celebrity. But he's MIA. Guess whose house will be next on the vultures' list?"

"Oh. Right."

"You'll have news vans trying to get in thru your **chimney**. Double file."

Jimmy paused.

"What is it?"

"Can't hurt my brand. Meaning, the exposure."

"**This** is the kind of exposure you want?"

"No, of course not. But **I** didn't do anything wrong. Might as well offset the suffering I'm subjected to on account of Tommy the Titbrain."

"Best of both worlds?"

"More like making lemonade."

"The protector of the prairies. The savior of the soil. The sprayer of bug bombs. The slayer of weeds come to do us harm. My fat, pimply **ass!**"

"I pray to Mars up among them stars you have a good reason to spew at me like you just did, son-in-law number five. Coz if you don't, you and I are thru."

"What's in them barrels next door?"

"Barrels next door? In the fuel depot?"

"Yes. The depot sheltering fuel."

"You gotta sacrifice to fly, Randy old boy. Gas and pesticide. What else?"

"What else?" Randy reached into the duffel bag sitting at his feet and took out a Strechler® X9 pistol. "Remember the day you gifted this thing to me? This nine-millimeter masterpiece of beauty and balls? My fortieth b-bash, the ol' four zero grande. Pride like that? I don't reckon I felt it ever in my whole damn life before or after. And I count the births of my young'uns in there." He pointed the gun at Dale. "Now? Now all I sense is the foul odor of perfidy."

"You're pointing a gun at another humanoid, there, sonny. That **alone** is a felony."

"Hmm . . . 'Of Pointings and Felonies.' Let that be the name of your book. The one you'll write while rotting in prison."

"The title might need some work."

"No worries there." Randy shrugged. "Staring at them gray walls will help jog them gray cells."

"Should I put my hands up?"

"You ain't even asking why I'm fuming coz you already know. Typical busted-perp conduct."

"I'm just standing here, trying not to get blown away by my own gift, dearest son-in-law."

"Purely a containment measure. I'll only use it if you up and lunge."

"Oh, there won't be any lunging done by these here dusty bones. Have we just met?"

"Well, I witnessed your silo ninja act not too many moons ago. Plus, you've just emerged from fighting off old fire and flame. Or at least pretending to."

"I came in here to grab my sleeping bag. I need serious shuteye before flying outta here."

"No sleep for the wicked." Randy gun-pointed at the office door. "Walk."

"To the depot?"

"Walk!"

Kerry pointed at the glove box. "Open it."

Jimmy popped it open to reveal a tranquilizer gun.

"ETA in five minutes. Abandoned dockyard. Based on heat signatures, he's holed up in there by himself. We could have stormed the place, but we figured better to trot **you** out first, try to make him come forth drama-less."

"Will do my best."

"Please do. I don't wanna tranq his ass, but if he gets too . . . animated, I'll have no choice. These tranq shots? An adult male is out cold within six seconds. It's part of our procedure. Tranq and conquer, as the kids say."

"Those kids. So smart these days."

"We never should've allowed them on the Internet. Now look."

Jimmy smiled. "I wanna laugh, but I can't. Things are . . . dawning now."

"You feel like a turd?"

"No. I mean, **you're** taking **me** there, not the other way around. Not like I sold him out. Still, something feels slimy about it."

Crowbar shook his head. "What other choice do you have? You're doing the only right thing here. Cooler heads. Brighter future. Well, future period."

"Some future for my brother. Rotting in a cell."

"Beats burning in hell."

Farmer Dale slowpoked his way across the hangar with Randy following ten feet behind.

"You know what did it, Dale? How I got wise to your little scheme?"

"**You've** got the gun, son-in-law no more. If you wanna talk, who am I to stop you?"

"The truck. The goddamn We Haul Gas® truck. You see a gas truck sprawled on your land in the middle of the night and you figure **rustlers?** That pig ain't flying, Dale! That pig ain't flying as hard as it might try, straining its sweaty mug and flapping its stubby little swine hooves."

"I think **you're** the author in **this** family, Randy of House Hofstetter."

"**Hendricks.**"

"It was dark."

"Eh?"

"Middle of the night, as you said. That's why these beady little eyes of mine didn't figure it for a fuel truck."

"The damn thing has a white body with green letters! Every man, woman, and child in Athenia knows what a We Haul Gas® truck looks like!"

"When it's in front of them, not while they're doing loops in a bug plane."

"Hold your tongue, serpent. You 'figured rustlers' so you could alert the Ministry and not the fire teams, giving them flames a head start."

"Here's a balloon-popper for ya: if I was behind the fire, why report the truck at all? Not like anyone knew I flew over it."

"To save the trucker, I suppose. You didn't want him on your conscience. Or to add murder to your rap sheet in case the scheme fell apart. One thing I ain't clear about: were the cops in on it? The ones who pulled him from the truck."

"Yes they were, and so was my dead granny, live via satellite from the nether realm. In fact, me and the whole of Lower Herzland conspired to mess with the head of Randy Hendricks. Boredom? Busted!"

Dale reached the entrance to the airstrip fuel depot. "And because you 'got wise' to our devious doings, there's a prize waiting behind this door."

"What was your reward? And who dangled it in front of your hooter? The Magma suits?"

"I'm a tired old man."

Randy took a step closer, raising the gun. "What does **that** mean? You admit what you did? Burned down your own land for thirty pieces?"

"Take it as you will, former son-in-law."

Randy grinned. "Let's have a smell, shall we?"

Dale opened the depot door and walked over to a set of barrels in a corner.

Randy made sure the safety was on and then put the Strechler® in his jacket pocket before following Dale in. "Let's not mix guns and gas. But if you blink funny, I'll stuff them rotten old bones of yours down this here sewer shaft."

An electric sound rang out and Randy collapsed to the floor.

Dale exhaled his second titan-type sigh of the day and leaned against a barrel. "Where the hell were you?"

Sigma stepped out of the shadows and took off his firefighter's helmet. "As the man said, guns and gas don't mix well."

"Funny man. What did you hit him with?"

"Sticky shocker. He'll be out for hours."

"Brave new world."

"How did you know he might be trouble?"

"I've known him since he was a tot. Before he ever married into the clan, obviously." Dale took a few steps to where Randy was splayed out and foot-poked his arm. "He agreed to livestock duty, easy-peasy. That made me queasy."

"He's normally not a fan?"

"Hates it with a passion. He's known far and wide for it. I just **knew** he'd show up here, drama school style. Felt it in my guts."

"Good thing I stuck around, eh?" The phony firefighter shook Dale's hand, then scooped the sticky shocker off the floor. "Do you have a ride out of here?"

"I do, but I'm drained beyond repair. Can you call someone?"

"You can piggyback on the helo they're sending for me."

"Thank you, Sigma. Again."

"What about Sleeping Beauty here?"

"Feed him to the fire."

"Ready?"

"Who's ever ready for something like this?"

"The tech helps." Kerry showed Jimmy the Heatwave™ screen attached to his inner forearm.

"I meant . . . you know, mentally."

"Just keeping the convo light." Kerry pushed open a rusty, dusty, crusty double door with a mega squeak. A beam of moonlight shone thru a hole in the roof.

"**Tommy?** Kerry Douglas, United Vigilance! I come in peace, please believe! Jimmy is right here next to me, all worries and jitters!"

Ten ticks of silence.

"How did you know I was in here?"

"My trusty heat sensor, see?" Kerry waved his arm at the darkness of the cavernous warehouse in front of them. "Dot marks the spot!"

Five more ticks of silence.

"Dots in the darkness, eh? That's all we are in the end."

Kerry and Jimmy exchanged looks. "Sure, Tommy, I can see your point!"

"Is there a sniper team with ten thousand gleaming shafts outside?"

"We do have backup, but there's no need to involve them! Just come out and talk to us!"

A clang ricocheted off the warehouse walls, making Kerry and Jimmy jump.

"Don't shoot. I'm coming out."

Tommy emerged from the darkness but remained at a distance of about thirty feet. "Awfully quiet, there, hermano mio. Ain't your job to talk sense into me?"

"Tommy, we share a brain—practically. But god**damn,** what were you thinking? I mean, I don't even know how to ask this question. It's beyond insane."

"What question?"

"What—**you burned a man to death!** For what, ordering the wrong kind of donuts? And not just any man. Oh no, Tommy Lo shoots for the stars, don't he?"

"I didn't know he'd turn out to be a big kahuna. In fact, no one was supposed to get hurt. I just meant to scare the owners."

Jimmy stepped forward. "But **why?** And why with a frickin' flamethrower?"

"I blame you."

"**This** I gotta hear."

"Always holding me back, derailing my dreams, using me however it best suited you." Tommy raised his index finger to pump up the scolding. "Every time I forgave. And every time I got burned harder."

"You're a grown man, brother. We rise and fall by the choices we make."

"You **have** your brand. You're the WUWI guy, adored by thousands. Prob'ly millions soon. And what do **I** got? This stupid stunt." Tommy shook his head. "I saw it as a way to get my own brand going. On the streets, you know? 'Fuck around with Tommy Lo, and he'll show up with flames at your door.'"

Jimmy and Kerry exchanged another look.

"Enough with the glance exchange!" Tommy snapped. "What, it wasn't the best of plans? Yeah, no kidding. I know that now too! Sure as shit not as cunning as some of **your** devious schemes! Like the way you tricked Pops into signing the house over to you. Right before ass-kicking him into Fogieland. He ain't even sixty yet."

"Retirement community. Where he continues to thrive."

"It's all an act. Pretending it was his idea. Feeble attempt to preserve his last shred of dignity."

Jimmy turned to Kerry. "Ever notice how 'shred of' is only used with 'evidence' and 'dignity'?"

Kerry smiled but kept his eyes on the tips of his shoes.

"Or the way you squeezed me out of WUWI—**my** brainchild, by the way—without a cent of buyout dough."

"I did invite you to come back."

"As an employee! A goddamn **employee!**" Tommy stepped forward, and Kerry took out the tranq gun.

"No need for this, brother. Let's all walk outta here—" Jimmy stopped and squinted at Tommy, who now stood closer to him than at any other point of the night. "What's different about you?"

"Had a little work done on the old muggo to gogo." Tommy did a circular motion around his face. "To make sure I'm a dead ringer for my favorite twin."

Kerry fired a tranq shot above Jimmy's collar—the WUWI star clutched his neck, wobbled, and keeled over.

"Bye-bye, brother." Tommy stepped into the light. "If you bump into Satan, maybe you can trick him out of his throne, become the new ruler of hell."

13 Curtain

"The body of Thomas 'Tommy Lo' Lorenz, the prime suspect in the Donuts or Nothing® flamethrower attack, was discovered this morning in East Nudwick, a suburb of Athenia City. So far, the police have ruled it a suicide, while noting that the investigation is ongoing. Here's Flip Johnson with the latest."

"Lin, I'm standing here in front of what used to be a dockyard. This morning, right around sunrise, a jogger spotted a strange sight on his regular route. After taking a closer look and realizing it was a human body, he called the police. As you can see, a multitude of law enforcement vehicles are behind me as both the East Nudwick and the Athenia City police have converged on this location. The body has been identified as that of Tommy Lorenz, but his cause of death is yet to be determined."

"Flip, the police have preliminarily ruled it a suicide. Any updates on that?"

"According to people close to the investigation, no evidence of any third-party involvement has been uncovered yet. Tommy had no phone among his possessions—presumably to avoid any digital traces that could lead to his hideout—but the police did find a portable radio. The working theory is that Tommy heard the radio broadcast naming him as a suspect and saw no other way out of his predicament."

Esteban Estez muted the box. "Check to the mate once again."

"Eh?" Hugo Jimenez looked up from where he was adding extra sugar to his ForzaPressa™-concocted coffee. "Don't tell me **we** had something to do with this."

The viscount shrugged. "He who wishes to keep his tax dough must not succumb to a doubter's moonglow."

"Double eh?"

"You got your java and pretzels?"

They were having either late breakfast or early brunch in the Schloss Estez* second-floor salon. Sitting on a couch, the host had his feet up on a wooden coffee table with his plate and java perching on the armrest.

"One last stir." The lawyer tap-tap-tapped the plastic spoon on the cup lid and then discarded it into an empty Get It Twisted™ Baker Bunker Bag™, which now doubled as a trash bag. He grabbed his coffee and overflowing-with-pretzels plate and took a seat on a tufted leather armchair to the left of Esteban's couch.

"I couldn't involve you in this one." The viscount bit off a pretzel piece and pointed at the muted box. "You had too much on your plate—pun!—with taking over the Channel 5® group, plus dealing with Harrington, on top of all your day-to-days. Not to mention discovering what it feels like being a billionaire. Quite frankly, I'm puzzled you still wanna lawyer on. But I appreciate it."

"All in a day's work. I consider you a brother."

"Ditto." Estez raised a coffee cup. "Something about fires and hell?"

"All will be swell."

They laughed and touched plastic.

"Cinnamon AndThenSome®. Yum!" The viscount squashed the empty cup. "You wanna know how it all ties together, Bulby? You want a peek behind that velvet curtain?"

"I'm just curious."

Estez cocked a brow.

"Fine. I'm burning to know. Being behind the eight ball hurts my soul."

"There you go." Estez finished off a pretzel. "I was thinking just the other day . . . Ten years ago, me, Sigma, and the boys were scoping out the Barton place.* Winter in Konnorka. The only thing more frozen than my ass was my balls."

Hugo burst out a laugh, spilling some of his coffee.

"But I had this dream, Bulby. This fire ripping my chest apart. To rise above the mud. To snatch those distant stars. To take the hand fate dealt me and throw it back into its stupid face."

"And you did. With a vengeance."

Estez pulled a distance-gazer while sipping coffee from his second cup.

"Speaking of vengeance . . ." Jimenez shifted in the armchair. "That convo you had with Ox at the stadium, did you trade vengeance for pipeline?"

Estez nodded. "People's brains get clouded by vendetta fumes. Might as well put it to good use. Yorba Woods will get a bigger chunk of the new energy infrastructure."

"How will that help with taxes?"

"For that part of the equation, we need to shift our gaze toward the heart of our nation."

"Herzland?"

"Farmer Dale's® farm, Lower Herzland."

"The one going up in flames?"

"They'd been teetering on the edge of bankruptcy for the past five years. All Dale needed was a nudge."

Hugo un-slumped himself. "He burned down his own farm? For the insurance money?"

"What choice did he have? The Magma mafia was offering him a pittance for the pipeline passage. Plus, we framed We Haul Gas® for it. People are so mad at them, now they'll side with RED ORE® on any major energy policy change."

"Was the driver in on it?"

"Nah. Simons and Paulson from the local AUIM slipped a muscle relaxant into his coffee and jammed up his comms, allowing them to remotely steer the truck off the road. We could have used a lethal substance just as easily. On the driver. This way he still got to go back home to his kids, albeit banged up."

"He'll still have to stand before the judge for falling asleep at the wheel."

"The Ministry guys also busted up a road chunk, making it look like the truck hit a section damaged in the storm."

"The dawn of a kinder, gentler viscount?"

"Here I am, brunching pretzels. Anything's possible. Before you ask, the pretzel thing was a happy bonus. Tim Phillips came up with the prison escape caper to secure passage thru Kelski's land. I knew Leo was struggling, and I figured I'd throw him a bone by having the guys vamoose in one of his vans. Leo will use the windfall to grab Aurelia agri-land so we'll be in on the ground floor of the new farm frontier. Should come in handy."

"What is Simons' and Paulson's reward?"

"The major* will take care of them. A combo of rank and cash, I'm sure."

"Good to have friends in high places."

"Not high so much as right."

"Corrigan was in on the escape?"

"Yes. Padding his retirement fund. Worth his weight in gold, old Oscar. They don't make 'em like that anymore. The escapees made their way into Kelski's house while the old man was out chopping wood or something. Klenny, his nephew, knew a way into the basement that didn't require breaking in. Prior to the convicts arriving at the homestead, Simons sent Kelski's guard dog to dreamland with a good old tranq shot."

"Down, doggie."

"We'll pay each of them a hundred K for every year that gets tacked onto their original sentences due to the escape."

"Only fair. They won't blab?"

"All they know is they had to escape in that pretzel van, hide in Old Man Kelski's basement, and wait for the cavalry to arrive. What would they blab about? The money? Well, if they do . . ." The host made an air noose.

"They won't blab for long."

"Oh, before I forget, funny story. I guess." The viscount rubbed his hands together to expel the pretzel crumbs. "Sigma was liasoning with Dale. He had to think on his feet when Dale's son-in-law sniffed out the scheme."

"How?"

"He realized Dale sprayed a non-detectable fire accelerant instead of pesticide. After the AUIM got the trucker out, Dale went to the crash site and ensured the truck ignited. Plus, he delayed calling in the fire."

"What did he do to the son-in-law? Sigma."

"Zapped the prick with a sticky shocker."

"Like a bolt from beyond."

"Then he dumped the body where fire gobbled it up. Unfortunate accident." Estez finished his second cup. "Anyway, Yorba Woods will take in the refugees from Herzland and give 'em jobs on the pipeline construction. I expect about a quarter of them to accept our warm bosom, mostly young families. We'll build housing for them. New schools, shpitzes. Dare I say, pissoirs."

"Gotta have those."

"In return, we get to keep all our tax moolah. Every last cent. In perpetuity."

"Consider my jaw dropped. But how will the locals take the influx?"

"Once they realize their tax bill has been halved? Once they wake up to literally thousands of new job openings? They'll be too busy buying furs and popping whoorz to complain."

"You mentioned Phillips. A keeper?"

"He did well. Gave us inside intel on LRO. Sussed out the rat in RED ORE® thru a mole in the Board, thereby reaching eleven trust level with Ox, which allowed him to recommend yours truly for roach quash duty."

"How did Luke O'Reilly enter the fray?"

"When our dear friend Neil Zorich broke into WARLOCK®,* he started attending sponsor schmooze events. At one such event, a certain furniture heiress caught his wandering eye."

"Anna Olkin."

"Completely and utterly kertwanged his brain, that one. Anna Olkin this and Anna Olkin that. There was only one problem."

"Unlucky Luke."

"Two birds with one stone sitch, if there ever was one. The tricky part was offing Luke. It had to be so public, so over the top that the O'Reillys would be forced to seek Rick Wrecker®-style justice no matter what they thought of their troubled tyke."

"How did you get Tommy Lorenz to pull the flamethrower stunt?" Hugo asked, glancing at the box.

"Counter question: who'd be willing to pull a stunt like that and hope to get away with it?"

The lawyer mini-mulled it. "Someone with a bad case of twin grudgery."

"Bingo, baby! Kerry knew the brothers from where all of them grew up together, up on Levski. One day he bumped into Tommy at a corner store. Tommy proceeded to spill his guts about Jimmy's latest spurn. Kerry saw the greed in his eyes and the hurt in his heart. Same as with Dale. All it took was a nudge."

"What became of the flamethrower?"

"He dumped it under wet cement on the northern edge of the construction site, then got in his van and drove to Nudwick."

"How was the body switch made?"

"Kerry brought Jimmy over to Tommy's hideout—the old 'make him listen to reason' ploy. While the brothers were talking, he hit Jimmy with a tranq shot. Then he and Tommy carried the body to the roof and threw it to its splat."

"How much are you paying Tommy?"

"Zilch. He'll live as Jimmy from now on, making big bunce with WUWI. You know how many new subscribers signed up? Two frickin' million. It's the biggest thing in streaming since that actress's sex tape broke."

"Everybody and their mother wants to hear what Tommy Lo's brother has to say."

"I'm sure a lot of those people will stick around only briefly and then unsub. But the cheapest plan is one zaler per week, so he'll pocket two mil within a week at the absolute minimum. Plus he gets his house back."

"Hang on, won't the cops triple-check to make sure the 'right' twin is dead?"

"Ever hear of the White Wizard?"

"From Doomers of Gloom® or something?"

"Nah, the dentist. Owns franchises."

"Oh, **that** guy. I've seen him on TV."

"He got wiped out during one of Kerry's Ring of Ruin nights. To erase the debt, Kerry asked for a five-minute access to his client database." The viscount took a sip from his third and final cup of coffee. "Kerry's tech guy switched Tommy and Jimmy's records."

"Did the Wizard ever ask why Kerry wanted access?"

"Not once. According to Kerry, the guy agreed within two seconds. As long as it gets him back to that card table."

"Fucking degenerate."

"If you've got that busted gene, the lure of the zock siren is irresistible."

"Didn't Tommy have a criminal record? In addition to a dental one?"

"Minor stuff, but yeah, he did."

"What about fingerprints?"

"Crowbar lifted Jimmy's prints after tranquing him. He gave the data to Battaglia, who uploaded those prints in place of Tommy's."

"Battaglia, the lead dec? He was part of it too?"

"Of course. He's the guy who won the game against the Wizard, walked away with a fortune. You think he won fair and square? The room was dotted with mini-cams. One of Kerry's guys was feeding him info on other players' cards."

"Hot damn, that is one delicious piece of devilish deviosity!"

The viscount downed his cup.

The End

Planet Kyzer

Had he been born 200 years earlier, author Kris Kyzer would likely have amassed an army of merciless mercenaries, taken over a small country, and established his own glorious nation. There, he would have dispensed all manner of pleasures to his subjects—and all sorts of plan-foilery to the enemies of his realm. But we live in different times, so instead of all that jazz, he writes books filled with grasping puppet masters, debased politicians, predatory moneymen, unhinged kingpins, and unscrupulous cops—all chasing grand schemes and warped dreams in the slime and grime of the Athenian Union. Plus humor. You gotta have humor.

Today, Kris spends his days in the Great White North, where he enjoys swimming without sharks and feeding his delusions of grandeur.

Hail Kyzer!

Printed in the USA
CPSIA information can be obtained
at www.ICGtesting.com
CBHW030249081024
15373CB00046BB/912